1924

A LADY OF LETTERS

Also by Jacqueline Diamond

Lady in Disguise
Song for a Lady

A LADY OF LETTERS

— Jacqueline Diamond —

WALKER AND COMPANY

NEW YORK

First published in the United States of America
in 1983 by the Walker Publishing Company, Inc.

Published simultaneously in Canada by John Wiley & Sons
Canada, Limited, Rexdale, Ontario.

Library of Congress Catalog Card Number: 83-5813

Printed in the United States of America

10 9 8 7 6 5 4 3 2 1

Library of Congress Cataloging in Publication Data

Diamond, Jacqueline.
    A lady of letters.

    I. Title.
PS3554.I24L34 1983   813.'54   83-5813
ISBN 0-8027-0741-6

For Kurt

=1=

MARIANNE STROLLED DOWN the gravelled path through the rose garden, reading and rereading the letter. Excitement welled up in her so that she could scarcely breathe.

"My dear mysterious Mata," read the familiar bold masculine writing. "I cannot convey to you my joy at learning that you are to come to London, and that in the course of your visit here you may make yourself known to me. Greatly as I admire your poetry, and deeply as I have enjoyed our correspondence these last months, I had not dared to hope I might have the honour of meeting you in person."

There was more, commenting with admiration on her latest poem in the *Gazette*, and then the closing, signed only, Your Humble Servant, J.

Your Humble Servant. Quite clearly, from the heavy cream paper and the elegance of the footman whom her cousin Will had seen delivering one of the letters at the *Gazette* offices, he was no servant at all. The J—was it his first initial or his last? James, perhaps, or Jonathon, or Mr. Jones?

She had feared, when she wrote that she was to come to London for the season, that he would not wish to meet her, perhaps would end their correspondence entirely. Now she could scarcely bear to delay a moment, and only her eighteen years of proper breeding kept her from throwing back her head and shouting with happiness.

The lowering angle of the sunshine over the leafy rose bushes, already bud-swollen although it was barely March, drew Marianne back into the present, and she turned reluctantly toward her grandfather's house. It would never do to keep the fierce Lord

Jonas Marlow cooling his tea, waiting for a laggard granddaughter.

Even though she had lived here for three years, since the deaths of her cousin Will's parents, it had never occurred to Marianne to confide any of her wishes or hopes to her grandfather, and certainly not her secret identity as Mata. Only Will Sloan and his wife Celia knew that, for it had been necessary to have an intermediary in London to place the poems for her and forward correspondence addressed to her pseudonym. Besides, she could never keep secrets from Will; he had become the brother she'd never had.

Marianne hurried up the steps and paused in front of a hall mirror to pat her hair back into its chignon. She glanced ruefully down at her simple green muslin dress, with its soiled hem. It was well enough for walking in the garden, and brought out the emerald tint of her eyes and the silver highlights in her ash-blond hair, but it was hardly the thing for the drawing room. Yet if she stopped to change she would be late to tea.

Marianne glided noiselessly into the room, glancing quickly about the massive Palladian space that seemed so suitable to her grandfather. She herself always felt constrained by all the grandeur, the triumphal arch of a doorway and the carved and gilded ceiling. Still, the heavy velvet curtains had been looped back to allow the afternoon sunshine in.

Marianne perched upon the sturdy Chippendale chair. Her grandfather glanced up only briefly from where he sat conversing with Aunt Edith Marlow and her daughters, Lucinda and Jane.

The girls looked up, and Marianne noticed, not for the first time, how unlike they were. Lucinda—long-necked, chestnut-haired Lucinda, so proud of her elegant bearing, so contemptuous of her younger cousin's open ways—all but sneered at her, yet it would not do to be unfriendly to Lucinda.

It was only through Aunt Edith's generosity—with perhaps a touch of prodding from Grandfather—that Marianne was to have her come-out this spring along with Jane. Lucinda, with her two years of experience, would be vastly important in advising them of the myriad subtleties of pleasing the ton, the members of London's finest circles. Although, Marianne admitted to herself, there were times she longed to slap Lucinda's arrogant face.

Jane and Marianne exchanged glances, and were barely able to repress their giggles. The two had seen little of each other while growing up, but they found themselves possessed of a natural affinity. Little mouse-brown Jane, who kept her hazel eyes timidly focused on the floor in the presence of most people, laughed and chattered with Marianne, while, in her turn, Marianne found Jane one of the few relations besides Will with whom she did not have to watch her every word and gesture.

"We will have tea now," Lord Marlow told the butler, and nodded at the ritual response, "Very good, my lord."

Edith resumed speaking almost immediately. "Charles would not think it necessary, I am sure, Jonas."

"What my son thinks does not concern me, since he is in Dover." The earl stared through his quizzing glass in a manner that would have withered anyone less strong willed than his daughter-in-law. "*I* think it necessary."

"Oh, Mother, there is no cause to fuss," Lucinda said crossly. "If Grandfather wishes us to attend a ball in the country before we go to London, what objection can there be?"

"It is not that I object, Lucinda," said Aunt Edith in a tone of rebuke. "I merely fear that we have not brought the proper clothing."

"But he has alresdy accepted the invitation, has he not?" asked Jane shyly.

"Besides, Mother, I am sure we have sufficiently fine dresses for a country ball," sniffed Lucinda.

Their conversation was interrupted as a footman and a maid entered with the tea and cakes. Marianne had been listening idly but now, in the silence, her aunt's true meaning reached her and she flushed.

What Edith meant was that Marianne did not have sufficiently elegant clothing, and it was quite true. Grandfather had arranged to purchase a new wardrobe in London, but until then she had only her schoolgirl dresses.

"Perhaps I need not attend," she said when the last servants had gone. "It is true that I, at least, do not have the proper gown yet, and I shall not mind missing an evening with the Hounsleys."

"You can wear any of my dresses you like," Jane said. "Certainly you must come."

"Nonsense, Jane, she is much too tall and slender to wear your clothing," said Edith. "But I supose Lucinda has something or other she might borrow."

The older girl assumed a petulant expression, one Marianne was sure she never disclosed to her London acquaintance. After all, Edith had told them all that Lucinda had passed two seasons without a husband only because she could not bear to give up being the reigning beauty. Furthermore, Edith had said on more than one occasion, the Marquis of Whitestone—whom everyone knew to be the leader of society and a close friend of the Prince Regent—had distinguished her several times and was said to be on the point of offering for her.

"I suppose she could wear the rose sarcenet," Lucinda said grudgingly. "I find the colour does not look so well on me as I thought, and the style is, as the French say, *un peu démodé*."

"Do not overwhelm us with your generosity," said Lord Marlow with a trace of humour, and Marianne almost smiled as their eyes met briefly. Although her grandfather was never easy with her, he had always been fair—more than many members of the family.

"Jane, do not eat so much," Edith said as her younger daughter took a second cake. "You are too plump already. I fear you will not make so good an impression as your sister unless you are more careful."

And what kind of impression will I make? Marianne wondered, retreating into her own thoughts. I shall be decked out decently enough, and after all, I am the granddaughter of an earl. But how can I blame society if it cannot forget who my father is?

Jean-Pierre Arnet. A handsome emigré from the French revolution, a count, or so it was believed. He had established himself in trade, like so many of his countrymen who had fled to England to avoid the horrors of the guillotine.

Yet he maintained certain connexions among the English nobility, and so he had become acquainted with Mary Marlow, Marianne's mother. Despite the opposition of her family, Mary eloped with Jean-Pierre to Scotland, and afterwards the young couple was grudgingly accepted.

Marianne was their only child, but she scarcely knew them, for the requirements of her father's business frequently took him to the continent, to Holland and Germany and Spain. His devoted wife chose to accompany him, and so their little girl was handed off to boarding schools, spending her holidays with unwelcoming relations.

Then, when she was twelve, her mother's cousins, the Sloans, returned from India with their son Will, ten years her senior. The Sloans were delighted to have Marianne join them for the holidays, and Will encouraged her in her writing.

For three years she had a family. Then the older Sloans died in a carriage accident and Marianne came to live with Lord Marlow. Will, having married, went to London, where he could improve his skills as a painter by contact with the finest talents in England, but he and Marianne corresponded frequently.

Seeing Will again would make her visit to London even more enjoyable, but she also looked forward with much curiosity to the Marriage Mart, as they called the subscription balls at the exclusive assembly rooms at Almack's. She was to ride in carriages through Hyde Park, and go to Vauxhall Gardens, and attend all manner of balls and routs.

Above all, she was to meet J. After her poems started appearing in the *Gazette* under a pseudonym some months ago, he had begun writing to her, first in admiration of her poetry, gradually in a more personal vein as their letters revealed a striking compatability of thought and spirit. Now that she was going to London, a meeting would be arranged, perhaps at Will's. What did J. look like? Would he be disappointed in her, or she in him? Was he perhaps married—but if so, he had misled her badly in his letters, and she would not believe that of him. At the very least, they would be good friends, and at most . . .

"I am sure we should go to the Hounsleys'," Lucinda was scolding her mother. "Are they not good friends with Lord Whitestone? Supposing he should be there, and I should miss him."

"Nonsense," said Edith. "Lord Whitestone is at his estates in Essex. So I heard from Lady Cowper only last week."

"But Priscilla Land might be there, and I must know what she is wearing this season!"

Priscilla Land, Marianne recalled hearing, was Lucinda's rival for Lord Whitestone, although, Edith claimed, not a serious one.

"Well, perhaps . . . " Edith was giving way.

The butler entered with a letter on a silver tray. "Excuse me, my lord, but this has just come for you," he said.

"Very good, Shortley." Lord Marlow picked up the letter. "Does the messenger wait for a response?"

"No, my lord," said Shortley, and retired.

As her grandfather read the letter, Marianne watched his expression turn from idle interest to a frown, to open fury. What on earth could it mean? No doubt it was some business matter, and she would never learn the truth.

But she had guessed wrong. "That damnable toad!" cried Lord Marlow, rising to his feet. "He has no right! Patriotism indeed!"

This uncharacteristic outburst left all four women too stunned to speak for a moment. Marianne sat numbly; the word patriotism had given her a clue that the letter concerned her, and in a most unpleasant way.

It was a year after the Sloans had died, in 1812, that she and all the world had learned the truth about her father. Marianne's parents had paid an infrequent visit to her before stopping for a while in their London home and then travelling back across the Channel. No sooner had they left than a recently discharged servant, no doubt bent on revenge, had gone to the authorities to report that Jean-Pierre Arnet was in fact a spy for Napoleon.

At first, the statement was dismissed as having been manufactured out of spite. However, the servant had been able to provide details and, upon investigation, certain papers were indeed found to be missing from the homes of several top officials whom the Arnets had recently visited. It was suspected that Jean-Pierre's wife had aided him in the thefts.

With a price on their heads, the Arnets could never return to England. It was said that they were living now in Paris; Marianne did not know, for they never wrote to her. But the parents who had given her so little of themselves had shared their disgrace with her liberally. In fact, they had even given her an extra portion, for while they escaped scot-free, she remained in England, a reminder of the family's shame.

Her only hope lay in the fact the Napoleon was retreating before allied forces and might soon be overcome. Her parents would still have been traitors, but memories of war are short in times of peace.

At last Edith broke the silence. "May we know what the letter says and who it is from?" she asked.

"You may know. You may all know!" Grandfather stormed, looking up from the letter he had been rereading with growing rage. "It is from that damnable—excuse my language, Edith, but this is bloody infuriating!"

"*Who* is it from?" asked his daughter-in-law.

"It is from Whitestone!"

"Whitestone!" Lucinda went pale. "Has it to do with me?"

"To do with you?" he roared. "Why the devil should it have to do with you?"

"Now do sit down, Jonas, and tell us straight away what is going on," said Edith in her most matter-of-fact voice. "You will give yourself apoplexy if you continue in this manner."

"I should call the villain out were I a few years younger!" said Lord Marlow, but he sat down again. "Here. Read it for yourself."

"Edith took the missive and read aloud. " 'My dear Lord Marlow. A most distressing piece of news has reached me and I fear I must communicate my views to you at the risk of some offence, although I intend none to you.' " She looked up with a frown. "Well, that is not a promising beginning."

"Oh, Mother, do go on," said Lucinda.

" 'I understand that this season you intend to present to society your granddaughter, Miss Arnet, daughter of the infamous traitor, Jean-Pierre Arnet.' " Edith shook her head. "So that is how the wind lies."

Jane reached over and took Marianne's hand in silent sympathy. Lucinda glowered.

" 'While I generally do not take it upon myself to judge the morality of others, this is not a matter on which I may be silent,' " Edith read on. " '.As you may know, I was a captain of infantry on the Peninsula and saw my men die more than once when it was suspected that word of our plans had been smuggled to the other side. In at least one case, it is now believed Monsieur Arnet was responsible.' "

Marianne tried to swallow and had a very hard time of it. Men had died, young men had been slaughtered, because of her father's treachery. One could not blame their captain for hating Jean-Pierre. But what had she to do with this?

7

" 'This scum has been exposed, but he has escaped without punishment to live in the luxury he gained by his cruel acts,' " the letter continued. " 'It is even said that he has risen to a position of influence in Paris. It is said he has intimate knowledge of all that transpires in England, that he maintains spies in high places, which even the Foreign Office has failed to detect. But if anyone in England aids and abets these fiends, or at least keeps the secret of their identities, it must be the Arnets' only child.' "

"That's monstrous!" Jane cried. "It's unfair."

"Oh, do be quiet," snapped Lucinda.

" 'Even today, I have visited one of my men, who lost an arm and his vision because of Monsieur Arnet's villainy, and would be destitute were it not for a stipend I have provided. In view of these facts, my patriotism will not allow me to lend even the appearance of approval to Miss Arnet's participation in London society. Therefore, I advise you that should she come to London, I and all of my friends will shun her and those who attempt to present her to society. I regret the enmity this may cause between us, as I know you are blameless in this matter, but I must stand on my conscience. Jeremy Hanbridge, Marquis of Whitestone.' "

The room blurred through Marianne's tears. That one letter had crushed all her hopes. Lord Whitestone was a powerful influence in society, and such opposition as this meant her social ruin. She would never dance at balls, or visit the enchanting Vauxhall Gardens, or meet J.

"He shall not do this!" Lord Marlow boomed. "I will not stand by and see my granddaughter pilloried for something that is not of her doing."

"Would you have us pilloried instead?" cried Lucinda. "Mama, it will be the ruin of Jane and me. All my hopes—how could he do this?"

"There must be some solution," Edith said. She didn't look at Marianne, and the girl thought she could guess what her aunt was thinking. *She doesn't want me to go, but she's afraid to cross Grandfather.*

"We shall simply not go at all," Jane said. "We can find husbands well enough in the country."

"You may say so, because you have never been out in London!"

Lucinda stormed. "You have never even met Lord Whitestone. Oh, to be shunned! Mama, you must think of something!"

Marianne felt some coherence begin to creep back into her thoughts. She had known there would be snide remarks, nasty looks and slights, but she had never expected such a blow as this. It was so unjust! Still, she could not let the rest of her family suffer needlessly.

"I appreciate your concern, all of you, but the solution is simple," Marianne said. "I shall not go to London."

"You bloody well shall!" cried her grandfather, who had never used such strong language before in her presence. "I will not have my family snubbed by this arrogant puppy!"

"I agree with you that he is loathsome and cruel," Marianne said. "But one cannot avoid seeing that he is most unlikely to change his mind."

"That does not signify," said Lord Marlow.

"It signifies everything!" said Lucinda. "We shall be invited nowhere, and no one shall accept our invitations. We shall be denied vouchers to Almack's. No one would dare risk incurring the wrath of Lord Whitestone; he is Prinnie's friend, and Lord Byron's. He goes everywhere, and everyone admires him. We shall all be ruined. He will never offer for me, and I shall die an old maid."

"I will call him out!" said grandfather. "There is no other way."

"Duelling is illegal nowadays," Edith reminded him. "And he would not agree to fight you, anyway, so Charles would have to take your place. Do you want your only son killed? Do you? They say Lord Whitestone is a crack shot, and heaven knows Charles is not."

"Wait," Marianne said, pulling her thoughts together. "Perhaps there is a way out of this after all."

Everyone looked at her dubiously.

"I have no great desire to be presented to the queen, nor to make polite conversation and drink watery lemonade at Almack's," she said. "What I want is to go to London and see Will, and meet interesting people, and . . . perhaps some eligible young men."

"Yes?" Edith prompted hopefully.

"If Will is agreeable, I will go and stay with him and Celia," Marianne said, warming to the idea even as she spoke. "They will show me about, and introduce me to their set."

"Lord Whitestone would hear of it," said Lucinda. "He would shun us anyway."

"Then I shall go not as Marianne Arnet but as Marianne Sloan, Will's sister," she said. "I do not feel it would be dishonest, for the Sloans were my family for some years. I think I would enjoy it quite as much as having a formal come-out, and should I meet some young man, well, it will be time enough then to tell him the truth. And as they are only second cousins, the relationship is not well known. Do say yes, Grandfather."

Lord Marlow looked thoughtful. "It enrages me, that this cox-comb should exert such power over my family, should force us into such manoeuvres. It is my instinct to fight him with the last ounce of breath in my body."

"Now, now, Jonas, that will not serve," said Edith, already looking much relieved. "I have no doubt Lord Whitestone will come round. Surely he must knew that Marianne and Lucinda are related, and that has not stopped him from paying my daughter marked attention. No doubt he will offer for her, and then Marianne will be his cousin, and he can hardly shun her then, can he?"

"Oh, do say yes, Grandfather," pleaded Lucinda. "It's not fair to spoil my whole life—" She caught his glare and added quickly, "when Marianne herself has said she would just as soon stay with Will, and enter London more quietly. It will all come out the same, surely."

"But I shall miss having her with us," said Jane sadly.

"It is not at all the same, but if you are all agreed, I will not stand against you," said Lord Marlow. "Marianne, are you certain this is what you want?"

"Oh, yes, Grandfather," she said. "I can even ride to town with Jane and Lucinda, and they can come to visit me at Will's. And only think, my wardrobe will not cost you nearly so much!"

He smiled, and the conversation passed gradually on to the up-coming ball at the Hounsleys'.

They rose at last, and Marianne found herself drawn to look at the letter. How odious he must be, she thought, this marquis who could so easily destroy a young girl's position in society. She turned the letter over to read it again.

She froze in shock. There was no mistaking the bold masculine handwriting. Lord Whitestone—Jeremy Hanbridge—was J.

= 2 =

MARIANNE SPENT THE next morning composing letters. The first, and easiest, went to Will and Celia, explaining the situation and asking if it would be convenient for her to visit with them for several months.

She also enclosed her latest poem for the *Gazette*. Before sealing the packet, Marianne read the poem over thoughtfully.

> Beneath a tree the lovers lay,
> Brushed by the speckled shadow play,
> Blinking against the brilliant day.
>
> They lay as a painting in a frame,
> Dreaming a dream that had no name,
> And slowly left as twilight came.
>
> The cool night sighed when they had gone,
> Stroking its fingers through the lawn
> Where silver spiders met the dawn.

She had written it thinking of J. Now she felt a cold rush of resentment and hurt and misery. Would she ever be able to feel trusting again towards a man? Surely there had been no hint in any of Lord Whitestone's letters that he was capable of acting with such cruelty towards a girl who had done no harm to him nor anyone else.

It didn't matter, Marianne told herself. But she knew that wasn't true. Not that she had ever been like Lucinda, living for the admiration of others, feeling at home only in a gown that cost a

12

hundred guineas, with a roomful of young bucks waiting upon her. Still, although she would perhaps be able to taste somewhat the London life she had long dreamed of, she would have to do so carefully, in pretence.

Then, too, she must face the strong possibility that she would someday meet Lord Whitestone in person, and have to maintain decorum and civility while wanting to slap his arrogant face. He must never guess that Marianne Sloan was Miss Arnet, or her cousins—Will included—could well pay a high price for it.

The second letter was to Lord Whitestone himself, and Marianne nibbled at her quill for a quarter of an hour before she began to write. The first effort she discarded as too dramatic, hinting at some dark tragedy. She tried again.

"My dear J." She paused. How could she address him in this manner, after what he had done? Yet if she were cold, he would wonder at it, and perhaps seek to learn "Mata's" identity so he might resolve the matter, and that would be disastrous. She let the words stand.

"It is with deep regret that I inform you that my plans have undergone a material change due to circumstances not of my making." Well, that was certainly true. "I will not be coming to London this spring as I had planned." A sort of lie, perhaps, but she certainly would not be coming *as planned*. "Therefore I fear we shall have to postpone our meeting until"—until when?— "until a later time."

She must also explain why she could not correspond with him further. True, it might be safer to do so, but she feared her rancour would show, and furthermore she might unwittingly refer to something in London that would give her away.

"I will be absent from my home for some months, and so must suspend our correspondence during this interval." That was both true and plausible. "I deeply regret all that has happened." She signed it Mata, for Marianne Therese Arnet.

It was with relief that Marianne went in to luncheon. She spent the afternoon with her aunt and cousins, deciding on a wardrobe for the following evening, when they were to visit the Hounsleys and stay for the night.

Under other circumstances they would have spent more than

one night with the Hounsleys, but there would be some visitors from London. Marianne did not wish to be exposed to too intimate an acquaintance, which might prove awkward later.

"The rose will do very well," Edith pronounced as Marianne modelled the gown. "I shall have my abigail take a tuck here and there and no one will know it is made over. Shall they, Lucinda?"

Her daughter glared at the warning and said, "No, of course not, Mother, why should I mention such a thing?"

"Oh, I can hardly wait!" said Jane. "This is my first ball, and yours too, Marianne, isn't it?" Her cousin nodded. "I do hope I can find enough things to say. Do you think anyone will dance with me?"

"It is hardly likely that anyone would slight Lord Marlow's granddaughter," said Edith, and then bit her lip as she looked at her niece.

"Don't worry, aunt," Marianne said. "No one from London will know who I am, and the people who live hereabouts would never shun me. We must go early, so that hardly anyone hears our names announced, and then I shall be almost anonymous. And I shall live very quietly once I am in London, so I doubt I shall meet anyone again."

"We must hope for the best," Edith said. "Now I think it is time for tea."

They set off the next morning across the pleasant meadowed landscape of Wiltshire in the great carriage. The vista was subdued and easy, unlike the abrupt wooded heights of Marlborough Downs further south, and even Lord Marlow was lulled to sleep after a while.

The family alighted for luncheon in Ashton Keynes, consuming some cold roast chickens and ham with fresh greens and apple pie. The three girls took a brief walk afterward to settle their food.

"I must admit to some apprehension about tonight, cousin," said Lucinda as soon as they were away from the inn. "Someone might report to Lord Whitestone that you were with us."

"Nonsense!" said Jane, more sharply than Marianne had ever heard her speak before. "He objected to her being presented to society, not at the Hounsleys' country estate. To society means being presented at the Court of St. James, to the queen, and then taken to Almack's and the lot, does it not?''

Marianne frowned. "I can't very well use the name Sloan today, when some of our country friends will be present," she said. "Perhaps you should simply introduce me as your cousin Marianne.''

"Mother would not listen to me," Lucinda said. "But I told her we should not go tonight.''

Marianne sighed. "Grandfather would have been even more furious. But to tell you the truth, I am not eager for it either. Perhaps I should plead a headache.''

"Oh, no!" Jane protested. "This will be your only ball of the season! You must have at least one!''

"Well, I shall retire early," Marianne said.

They turned back, walking along a little stream. "I wonder where this goes?" said Jane.

"To London, just as we shall do! It is the baby River Thames. Now come along!" Marianne led the way, laughing.

Marianne's professed uninterest in the ball vanished the moment she entered the Hounsley home. On their way up to the third floor, the cousins couldn't resist a peek into the second-floor ballroom, and even in daylight it took their breath away. The room had been turned into a garden, the walls draped with green hangings, large potted trees arranged in groups here and there, and masses of flowers surrounded the wall sconces.

For a moment, Marianne found herself at an imaginary dance. She could hear the musicians playing from their balcony, perhaps something as daring as a waltz. She swayed in the arms of a handsome stranger; they spoke of poetry and art and music. He talked of . . . of all the things J. had written of in his letters. Unhappily, she returned her attention to her companions and joined them in ascending to their rooms.

Most of the London guests had arrived the day before and gone out riding, and the house was quiet enough for the newcomers to catch a nap. They gratefully accepted the suggestion that supper be brought on a tray; Marianne wanted to be noticed as little as possible, and Lucinda openly agreed with her.

But at last it was nine o'clock and the strains of a quadrille drifted up to them. Lucinda, her hair dressed *à la Grècque*, wore an underdress of sea-green silk and a silvery spider-gauze overdress embroidered with silver fleur-de-lis. With her striking chestnut hair, she was clearly the beauty of the group, Marianne thought, but felt no envy. She was glad to let someone else be the center of attention tonight.

Jane, as befitted a young lady who had not yet had her come-out, wore white muslin, with puffed sleeves and pink ribbons at the high waist and the hem. With a ribbon through her short curls, she looked no longer mousy, but fresh and appealing.

Marianne spared herself a quick glance in the mirror. Lucinda's abigail had arranged her hair in a high chignon with spring flowers, and a long curl trailed down onto her almost bare shoulders. The rose gown was a bit daring, not what she would have chosen, but she had to admit the color put bloom in her cheeks.

"I think we all look very well indeed," said Jane with satisfaction. "Are Mother and Grandfather ready?"

They were, and the family descended together. They were among the first, Marianne noted with relief.

The room filled up quickly, however, and soon it was difficult to move through the crush. Marianne danced several sets with her grandfather and some other gentlemen of her acquaintance, then retreated into a clump of potted trees.

From her vantage point, she watched Lucinda sparkle and laugh merrily as young men gathered around. It would be almost a shame when Lucinda married, she reflected, for flirting was clearly her outstanding talent. It was an education to watch her ruffle her fan provocatively, then half-turn toward one young man while tossing a teasing glance at another.

Miss Land, a tall, fair woman with a regal bearing and, from what Marianne could hear of it, a keen and not altogether kindly wit, was in fine spirits also.

Jane did not want for partners, and Marianne was glad. For herself, she tried to suppress a twinge of regret. It was enchanting to think of dancing in the arms of a romantic man, but she saw no one who fitted that description in her estimation. Surely she should not mind missing the balls in London.

"Oh, my dear, you should be dancing!" It was Lady Hounsley, a large woman who sailed down upon her like a ship approaching dock. She was rigged in a heavy gown of emerald-green lustring, with a matching turban, above which swayed a clutch of costly ostrich feathers.

"I . . . was merely resting for a moment," Marianne said, but her hostess had already seized her arm and was pulling her back into the crowd. In a trice, Marianne found herself on the dance floor with a gangly young man possessed of an outrageous blue-and-yellow-striped waistcoat and a brilliantly yellow coat with padded shoulders. As soon as the dance ended, Marianne excused herself and fled out onto the balcony and down the stairs to the garden.

Far better than pleading a headache would be to find a seat in some inconspicuous spot where she could listen to the music and enjoy the mild spring breeze. It was still early in the evening, and Marianne found herself mercifully alone. Just as she had hoped, she came upon a bench among the lilac trees, close enough to the house to hear the music.

Here her thoughts were free to travel to London, and quickly did so. She had never dared tell anyone but Will of her feelings about her writing—to be labelled a bluestocking was most undesirable for a young lady—but in truth she was more excited by the prospect of meeting writers and artists than she would have been by a roomful of princes.

Poetry had been at first a way to express her loneliness. Then Will had exclaimed over it as displaying a genuine talent, and encouraged Marianne to read works both current and ancient and improve her taste. It was also he who had suggested submitting the poems, and she had agreed, with the provision that she do so anonymously. Gradually her writing had come to be an essential part of herself, almost more real than the world around her, just as J. had come to be more real to her than any of the young men she encountered in the country.

Marianne heard a couple approaching and quickly began cooling herself with the painted fan that dangled from her waist. Someone glanced at her and, apparently persuaded that she was only taking a breath of air, passed on.

The evening began to chill and Marianne considered slipping back to her room. She stood, and then hesitated as the music changed to a waltz. The new dance was almost shockingly intimate—imagine actually being held in the arms of a strange man!—and, at Almack's, one required the permission of the haughty patronesses before one could take part. But at a country ball, waltzing was permissible even for young unmarried women, and Marianne and her cousins had practised the steps before coming.

She would like very much to waltz, to sway to those uplifting and exhilarating strains, but couldn't imagine doing so with any of the tedious men she had seen that evening. Marianne closed her eyes and let the music fill her. Gradually she began to move with the rhythm and, gathering her skirts with one hand, rose and whirled lightly around.

Suddenly she felt a firm masculine grip on her waist and hand, leading her through the movements of the dance. Marianne gasped and looked up.

Grinning down at her with boyish delight was the most handsome man she had ever seen. He was tall and dark, with features that might have been harsh save for the warm glow in his deep brown eyes. The pressure of his touch and his nearness left her momentarily breathless, and Marianne found herself relaxing and enjoying the dance.

Perhaps he was only a dream after all. Perhaps in a moment he would vanish as suddenly as he had come. But what might happen in the future had, surprisingly, ceased to matter for that delirious moment as they spun round in the moonlit garden, laughing together as at some unexpected, shared jest.

Finally the music died away. They danced for a moment longer and then slowly drew apart.

"I have not offended you, I hope?" the man asked, his quirky smile telling her he had no real fear of rejection.

"Not at all," said Marianne saucily. "I only dance with men to whom I have not been introduced."

"Truly? That is most unusual!"

"And they must come upon me unexpectedly in the moonlight, or I simply disappear," she teased.

"Do you meet many men this way?" His eyes shone with mirth.

"More elves than men," she said, and they both laughed. "Now, you must tell me what you are doing here, for you know it is not good *ton* for a gentleman to wander about unaccompanied."

"I fear I have misplaced my chaperone," he said lightly.

Marianne rapped his arm lightly with her fan. "You must guard your virtue, you know, dear sir. Of course, now you are with me, you are quite safe."

"I had hoped otherwise." He awaited her response with one eyebrow raised.

"How can I reply to that?" Marianne challenged, feeling as if fairies were dancing in her throat. This was precisely the sort of repartee she had looked forward to enjoying when she was in London, the matching of wits and humour with her intellectual equals and superiors. Who would have expected to encounter such a man at the Hounsleys' country estate?

"I have not seen you in London," he said more seriously. "I know I should remember you if I had."

"Oh, but I am a woman of many disguises," she said, not wanting the conversation to turn to awkward matters. "Here beneath the lilacs, I am a . . . a . . ."

"Sprite," he said.

"A sprite," she agreed. "In London, you would not recognise me at all. I might appear one day as a washerwoman, and another as a duchess. It does keep life interesting."

"You are enchanting," he said, taking her arm and leading her back to the secluded bench. "You must tell me who you are."

"Ariadne," she said. "Rosalind. Juliet. Anyone you wish."

The man held her hand between his and caressed it as if it were a precious thing. The dark eyes looked intensely into hers, and Marianne felt herself lean toward him, a weakness spreading through her limbs.

His mouth closed over hers with restrained longing, his lips pressing gently and his hand slipping around her waist. He pulled her close, and Marianne could feel his heart pounding through his coat of superfine.

Reluctantly, they parted, Marianne tingling with mixed joy and apprehension. Despite her teasing, one simply did not go about dancing with strange men, and a kiss was reserved for one's intended. What must he think of her?

"I had best go in now," she murmured, but he detained her with a touch.

"Please accept my apologies," he said. "It was the moonlight and the music. I intended you no insult. I shall never refer to it again, if you will only forgive me."

"It is as much my fault as yours," she said. "But while I may also lay blame on this enchanting place, if I do not go now I shall have no excuse at all."

"At least tell me your name," he said with such unaffected earnestness that Marianne felt a lump stick in her throat.

This was the dilemma she had hoped to avoid: meeting a man she truly admired, and being forced to decide whether to trust him enough to reveal her secret. The hounds take Lord Whitestone for doing this to me! she thought.

"Did I say something wrong?" the man asked quickly. "You looked so angry all of a sudden."

Marianne shook her head. "I warned you I was mercurial, good sir," she said, unable to keep the light tone as she gazed at him with longing. "You see—"

The swishing noise of an evening slipper on grass made them both look up as Priscilla Land sped around a tree and slid to a halt. Without losing her composure, she quickly assumed a look of mock petulance on her aristocratic face.

"I only wished to warn you that there is a wager about," she told the man without more than a passing glance at Marianne, who felt suddenly dowdy and much too young. "Mr. Trimble has wagered five pounds that you have gone off in a snit when you found neither Beau Brummel nor the Prince Regent was here."

The man shook his head disdainfully. "Poppycock," he said, and winked at Marianne over her head.

"Precisely what I said." Priscilla batted her eyes and angled closer to him. "Lord Sefton bet you only went out to check on your horses, while I told them . . ."

Her simpering patter and his evident distaste for her proved so amusing that Marianne had to clap one hand over her mouth to keep from giggling aloud.

"I told them I would find you waiting for me here, and so I have!" Priscilla finished.

"Odd sort of waiting," the man said. "Generally one finds the wait tedious, and the end of it welcome."

"Precisely," said the girl coquettishly, and then, the irony striking her, gave him a startled look.

Afraid she would laugh aloud and be quite rude, Marianne darted away through the lilacs, finally giving vent to her mirth when she was alone. She hesitated then, and considered going back, but with Priscilla hanging about, she was unlikely to have a moment's privacy with him.

We shall meet again, she told herself with sudden confidence. He will find me, and if he does not, well, I shall find him.

She returned to the ballroom, feeling much better than she had in several days. Even if they could not talk alone tonight, they would meet somehow in London. At least she could manage to give him her name and direction in London, and then there would be plenty of time to further their acquaintance.

But scarcely had Marianne made her way into the crowd than Lucinda grasped her arm and hissed, "Come here!"

She tugged Marianne into a corner and whispered urgently, "Lord Whitestone has arrived! You must plead a megrim and go upstairs at once! Jane says she will go with you, if you like."

"There's no need," Marianne said. "I shall go by myself." Then she thought of the man in the garden. If she departed now, how would he know where to find her? "But not just this moment. Surely with all these people here—"

"It cannot be avoided if you stay!" Lucinda pleaded. "Grandfather is very angry and threatening to make a row, and everyone's attention will be called to the fact that you are here. Once Lord Whitestone sees you, he will recognise you anywhere! You will not be able to show your face at the opera, or anywhere!"

"Oh, very well," Marianne said angrily. It was intolerable, but Lucinda was right.

"Come away now," Lucinda urged. "There may be only just time."

"What do you mean?" said Marianne as she was pulled once again through the packed room. "You said he was already here."

"So he is. But he has vanished for some minutes. In fact, there is a bet on it. Mr. Trimble says that he was angry because the prince is not present. In fact, he has wagered five pounds against Lord Sefton.''

Marianne went cold and numb. She scarcely noticed when someone trod upon her foot or when a glass of negus splashed against her gown. The man in the garden was Lord Whitestone. And he was J.

At last she escaped Lucinda's grip and fled unnoticed up the stairway. Alone in her room, she threw herself onto the bed and pounded her fists against the pillow in frustration and disappointment.

=3=

BY THE TIME she arrived in London, Marianne had devised a scheme. It was so outrageous that at first she shied from it, but it contained all the necessary elements: it would protect her family, it would permit her the freedom of London and, best of all, it would secure her revenge against the odious Lord Whitestone.

"Are you certain you desire revenge?" inquired her cousin Celia when Marianne was safely ensconced in the Sloans's drawing room. Marianne had never met Will's wife before, but she immediately liked the open-faced young woman who welcomed her with a warm smile. "I must own, it sounds from what you have related so far as if you would desire a reconciliation with Lord Whitestone."

"What I desire is to teach him a lesson," said Marianne.

"Are you being entirely honest with yourself?" asked Will. Her stocky cousin, who had greeted his newly-appointed sister with enthusiasm, poured himself a glass of sherry. "My impression coincides very nearly with Celia's."

"Here is the way of it," said Marianne. "It is all very well to meet a handsome stranger in a moonlit garden, and it is all very well to correspond with a stranger and to confess one's innermost thoughts. And were I the only one concerned, perhaps I should chance it and present myself in my true person to Lord Whitestone."

"Surely you are not attempting to protect *us*," said Celia. "I assure you, we do not cringe in fear of being shunned by Prinny's crowd. If we were that sort, we should never have taken you in at all, I'm sure."

"I suppose he has touched my family pride," Marianne confessed. "Perhaps deep down I am as angry as Grandfather, and

23

since a woman cannot challenge a man to a duel, I intend to challenge him in my own way."

"Pray enlighten us," said Will, settling down with the air of someone about to enjoy a comfortable coze.

"Far from hiding, I shall go everywhere and be seen with everyone," Marianne said. "I shall be at the theatre and in Hyde Park, at Almack's and at Vauxhall Gardens. Lord Whitestone shall encounter me wherever he goes."

"And you intend to engage his heart, and when he has declared himself, then you will reveal your true identity?" suggested Will.

"That is part of it, yes." Marianne sampled one of the delicious tea cakes. "But it would seem a heartless and deceitful scheme the way I have laid it before you, would it not?"

"I am certain it would not make him think well of you," said Celia.

"Here is the best part," Marianne said. "I have already three identities: as myself, as Mata, and as Marianne Sloan. What I shall have before this charade is finished is a dozen more."

Her cousins stared at her in surprise.

"In the garden, I told him I might turn up almost anywhere, as almost anyone," said Marianne, who had described that encounter with the omission of a certain kiss. "And so I shall. Perhaps one day I shall sell flowers at Covent Garden when he is attending. The next evening he might see me at Almack's, demure in a white gown. The following night I shall tell fortunes, dressed as a gypsy. I shall be so outrageous he will be in complete confusion, and when I peel away all the layers and reveal my true identity, he can scarcely accuse me of deceiving him, when he has known all along I was not as I appeared."

"But you will ruin your reputation!" cried Celia.

"I have none," said Marianne. "So far as the *ton* is concerned, I am nothing but the daughter of the traitor Arnet, and not accepted into polite society. So what have I to lose?"

"But he will meet you as Marianne Sloan on some occasions," Will pointed out, although his tone indicated he was far from appalled at this daring scheme.

"I shall say it, too, is a disguise, and then I shall have been entirely honest," said Marianne.

"Well, not entirely," said Celia.

"You must help me, both of you," said Marianne. "I shall have to secure costumes and practice my speech so it is suitable to whatever role I am playing."

"It will also be necessary to have someone look out for you," said Will thoughtfully. "Posing as a flower-seller or what-have-you is not without its perils. I will not have my cousin wandering unprotected on the streets of London."

This was an obstacle Marianne had not considered. "Have you any suggestions?" she asked.

Celia and Will exchanged glances, and both said at once, "Fritzella Crane!"

"Heaven help me, who is that?"

"She was my nursemaid," said Celia. "But I fear she's grown rather eccentric."

"She sounds ideal for my purposes," said Marianne. "Where does she reside?"

"In our attic," said Will.

"Your attic?" It was Marianne's turn to be surprised. "Is she a madwoman then?"

"No, no," said Celia, pouring herself another cup of tea. "We offered her a home—we could not turn her out, of course. She might have had a cottage in Suffolk or a small house of her own in Chelsea, but she would not. She said our attic would suit her well, and there she dwells. She does go out almost every evening, but we hardly ever see her. I suppose the servants do think her mad."

"A most unusual arrangement," said Marianne.

"No more so than having one's cousin arrive and pretend to be one's sister, and go about selling flowers in the street," said Will. "You should count yourself fortunate that we are not more conventional."

"I hope I shall never lack appreciation," said Marianne. "May I meet this Miss Crane?"

They readily assented and so, before she had even seen her own room, Marianne found herself ascending the narrow stairs to the attic. Will led the way with a branch of candles, for the staircase was quite dark.

Will rapped at the door and a female voice from within called, "Enter, please!" They stepped inside.

Marianne was surprised to find the sitting room designed in all the latest style, with delicate Regency chairs and reproductions of Egyptian pottery and carpets. Despite tiny windows, the place seemed quite bright and cheery.

"Miss Crane?" called Celia. "We have brought you a visitor."

"I am in the Oriental salon," called the same voice from an adjacent chamber.

The second room was entirely different from the first, designed in the style of the previous century. Chinoiserie predominated: oriental silk hangings, japanned chairs and tables, vases brush-painted with delicate scenery. Shuffling toward them, the palms of her hands pressed together with the fingertips pointing up-wards, was an elderly woman dressed in a curious garment. The floor-length robe, white-embroidered upon white, was fastened in front with oriental frogs, and had excessively deep sleeves. Mari-anne reflected that one might almost use them as pockets.

"Miss Crane," said Celia. "This is our cousin, Marianne Arnet, although she is known just now as Marianne Sloan."

"Names mean little on the canvas of history," said Miss Crane enigmatically, her small, alert eyes taking in Marianne carefully. The elderly woman, despite her somewhat beaked nose and peculiar manner, appealed to Marianne at once. "The Oriental is not concerned with the petty matters that absorb the English-man."

"But you are not oriental," said Marianne, accepting a seat.

"Oh, but I was." Fritzella Crane, whom Marianne now ob-served to be wearing embroidered silk slippers, poured pungent green tea into delicate white cups, each decorated with a scene from China.

"Miss Crane believes in reincarnation," Will informed Mari-anne. "She believes she has lived before."

"That is perhaps not the correct phraseology," said Miss Crane who, to Marianne's astonishment, proceeded to sit cross-legged on the floor although her joints issued a series of cracks and creaks worthy of the London mail hitting a pothole at full gallop.

"I beg your pardon?" said Marianne, so distracted by the noise that she could scarcely remember what Will had said.

"It is perhaps not correct to say I believe I have lived before," said Miss Crane calmly. "I know that I have. It is you, Mr. Sloan, who believe you have *not* lived before."

"Perhaps Marianne would be interested in hearing about your lives," said Celia, winking at her cousin.

"Indeed." Miss Crane took a sip of tea. "I have attempted to decorate each of my rooms to correspond to one of my previous existences, although it is not always possible. I have been an Egyptian princess, a slave girl in ancient Greece, a Christian martyr, a Chinese scribe, and a gypsy."

"I would like to be a gypsy," said Marianne. "Also a flower-seller and a serving-girl and an Incomparable and a poetess."

"She means in this life," Will interjected. He outlined the situation while the older woman listened attentively.

"There was a similar situation in Greece when I was there," Miss Crane said when he had finished. "A young man of one of the first families refused to marry his intended because her father was disgraced."

"What did she do about it?" asked Marianne.

"She was a weak cup of tea, in my view," sniffed Miss Crane. "She acquiesced without a murmur and consented to be wed to some fellow or other who deigned to have her."

"What about the man who refused her?"

"He altered his preferences—this is difficult to phrase politely," Miss Crane said. "In Greece, certain matters were seen rather differently than they are today. He, shall we say, relied on his male friends for companionship."

"But did he never marry?"

"I believe there was a token marriage, for the sake of the children," said Miss Crane.

"I would never consent to that!" Marianne set her empty tea cup down with more emphasis than she'd intended.

"We shall rub on quite well," said Miss Crane. "It will be my pleasure to assist you in any way possible."

At Will's suggestion, they decided to postpone further discussion until the following afternoon. Furthermore, Fritzella had an engagement that evening, about which she declined to elucidate them, so leave was taken warmly all round and Marianne went down to see to her unpacking.

A freckle-faced country girl named Rachel had been employed as her abigail, and she was already smoothing out the wrinkles in Marianne's gowns.

"We shall have to go to the shops tomorrow," said Celia decidedly, eyeing a faded blue muslin. "Your grandfather has provided a tidy sum for your purchases, and you will need a great deal."

"I do not think I will need much above a few day frocks," protested Marianne. "Rather, we should find a gypsy costume and other such disguises."

"You shan't need much of that, for Miss Crane has several trunks filled with bizarre costumes that should serve you quite well," said Celia. "And you will need more gowns than you expect. But tell me, please, Marianne, are you quite set on this mad scheme?"

"More so than ever," said Marianne, arranging beside her bed some of her favourite books: the new sensation, *Pride and Prejudice*, by an anonymous lady, and *Evelina* and *Camilla* by Fanny Burney, as well as poems by Byron and more serious works, Shakespeare, translations of Greek plays, and several histories. "I cannot disappoint Miss Crane, now can I?"

Her engagement with that lady was not until teatime the following day, so Marianne and Celia set out in the morning in the Sloans's calash for a visit to the shops in Bond Street.

They were handed down from their carriage by a shop assistant at the first location, and ushered inside with offers of chocolate, which they declined. As the day progressed, one shop blended into another in a whirl of apricot muslin and bottle-green silk, chip-straw bonnets and cashmere shawls.

One must, Marianne discovered, have half a dozen ball gowns —each costing easily 100 guineas—as well as riding habits, morning dresses, afternoon dresses, and walking dresses, all embroidered and beribboned and yet, in the Regency style, displaying a simplicity of line that hugged one's figure.

"It's said some ladies dampen their undergarments so the gowns will cling," Celia confided as they examined a satin-straw gypsy hat and a poke bonnet with ruffled lavender silk inside the brim.

"I should think that would be more in the way of a—a Cyprian, than a lady of quality," said Marianne, shocked.

"You would be surprised," Celia murmured. "The way some ladies conduct themselves would no doubt scandalise even the Haymarket duchesses, who I'm sure behave with more discretion even at their annual ball for the gentlemen."

"Annual ball?" asked Marianne.

"It is said the Haymarket ladies conduct their own celebration each year, a party for their male friends," Celia said impishly. "Why, I have heard one can see earls, marquises, even dukes."

She halted as the shop owner returned, and the conversation moved on to the merits of a daring hat *à la Hussar* versus a Pamela bonnet.

Even after the gowns were ordered and the measurements taken, the trimmings and ribbons selected and the bonnets chosen, Marianne was not allowed to rest except for a brief luncheon taken at a small coffee shop.

There were evening slippers and day slippers to be decided upon, and half-boots, and all manner of gloves and shawls, even down to cambric handkerchiefs.

Encountering a friend in a jewellery shop, Celia was drawn aside as Marianne examined a set of simple, gleaming white pearls. A tinkling of bells announced a new arrival, and she glanced up to see a stunningly beautiful woman glide through the door.

The lady was tall, with raven hair and piercing brown eyes but the fairest of complexions. Gowned in a blue velvet carriage dress, she appeared to be a countess, at the least.

"Miss Brinoli." The shopkeeper hurried forward.

"You recall the ruby earrings that were given me last month?" asked the woman haughtily, gazing around as if too proud to look the man in the face.

"Oh, yes, indeed, madame," he said. "They were made especially to the marquis's order."

Marianne strained to hear more, although she kept her eyes averted. If the lady was a marchioness, why had he called her Miss Brinoli?

"Lord Whitestone has instructed that I be made a necklace to match," Miss Brinoli said.

Marianne turned and stared. Lord Whitestone wasn't married. This lady, then, was no lady at all, but his mistress!

"There is no need to gawk, girl," snapped the woman.

"Pardon me," murmured Marianne. "I did not mean to stare." She turned away, feeling herself flush. It had never occurred to her that the marquis might have a mistress. J. had certainly never mentioned such a thing, but then, why would he?

She had heard, of course, that gentlemen in London frequently kept ladybirds, but she had never imagined one would be as beautiful as this. With a sinking sensation, Marianne began to wonder if she would truly be able to fascinate the marquis as she had planned.

Espying the woman, Celia instructed Marianne to return the pearls, and they left hastily for another jewellery shop.

"The temerity of that woman!" Celia gasped when they were on the street. "Parading herself about like a respectable soul!"

"She is Lord Whitestone's mistress, did you know that?" asked Marianne.

"However did you . . . well, never mind." Celia sighed. "Yes, I had heard. She was a minor singer at the opera. Serena Brinoli. She pretends to be Italian, and perhaps she had some ancestors from Italy, but she comes from Liverpool and her greatest accomplishment is no doubt the amelioration of her accent."

"But does he pay all her expenses?" asked Marianne. "How does such an arrangement work? Must she see only him? What if there were children?"

"Marianne!" Celia looked at her in horror. "You should not even know of such things."

"But I do, and I have always wondered—"

"Then you shall wonder a while longer."

Although Celia was not more than a few years above Marianne's age, she was a married woman and must know a great deal more of the world, her younger cousin reflected sadly. Why was it that when a woman married and was initiated into all these mysteries, she inevitably joined the silent conspiracy to keep younger, less fortunate women in ignorance?

The two shared a delicious tea of cream cakes and biscuits. Will was painting at his studio, and he and his wife were to spend the evening at a small dinner for artists. Since Marianne's arrival had come a few days earlier than anticipated, she had not been invited; but it did not signify. She was more than happy to pass the evening in the unpredictable company of Fritzella Crane.

She found that lady wearing a simple shift made from some rough burlap, her graying hair pulled into two incongruous braids.

"I cannot guess what period this is," said Marianne, perching upon a little Regency chair. "Pray enlighten me."

"It is the year 1215, in France, but that is of no moment," said Fritzella grandly. "It is a sure sign of the poseur to believe that he or she lived only in colourful times, as important people. In many lifetimes I was merely a peasant, and that is what I represent now."

"How many lifetimes have you lived?" asked Marianne, intrigued.

Miss Crane waved her hand dismissively. "Whenever I think I have counted them all, I have a dream or a flash of memory and I recall another," she said. "Some of them are quite scandalous."

"Tell me about them."

"Indeed I shall not," said Miss Crane. "Whatever I may have been in previous centuries, I am not lost to propriety in this one."

"Then we should get on with our planning," said Marianne. She briefly considered suggesting that they attend the Cyprians' ball, but decided in light of their last few remarks that the time was inopportune. Moreover, after seeing the beautiful Miss Brinoli, she was not at all sure she wanted to present herself to the marquis in the vicinity of such notable competition.

"One of your suggestions appealed to me particularly," said her companion. "That was of going to Vauxhall as a gypsy girl. I was a gypsy once, you see, and have costumes enough for the two of us."

"Will you show me how to read the cards?" asked Marianne eagerly. "I could tell his fortune!"

Fritzella shook her head. "Do you think this is a game, girl? The Tarot is not a toy."

"Then how shall we proceed?"

Miss Crane leaned forward in her seat, her eyes sparkling with youthfulness under the grey hair. "I shall tell the fortunes, and you shall be my assistant. You shall fetch the gentlemen to me."

"Do you know Lord Whitestone? Have you ever met him?"

"I have seen him," Miss Crane said ambiguously. "He is known in society, is he not?"

"Would you tell my fortune?"

Fritzella considered. "I am not suitably attired."

"Oh, please! I should so love it, and how can I be your assistant when I have so little idea what I am assisting?" Marianne eyed her companion hopefully, trying to suppress a nagging fear that all might not come out as she hoped. Suppose the cards revealed . . . revealed what? What was it that she secretly feared?

The elderly lady stepped out of the room, closing the door quietly behind her. It was some minutes before she reappeared, dressed in a simple but quite respectable black cotton gown, with her hair pulled back in a chignon. In her hand she held a deck of curiously painted cards.

"Is it like our usual deck?" asked Marianne, peering at the cards and making out faded splashes of colour and some human figures.

"Only superficially," said Miss Crane. "The number of cards in the Tarot may vary, but I use the genuine Italian deck, and there are seventy-eight cards. Of these, fifty-six are divided into four suits, not unlike your playing cards. The others form the mysteries, and I shall not explain them to you, for your interest is not that of the true mystic."

Marianne sat back, feeling slightly rebuffed, and also very curious. Where did Miss Crane slip off to each night? Had it anything to do with her cards, or with reincarnation? Celia had called her eccentric, but there might be something deeper here. Yet whatever it was, it was not evil, she felt quite certain.

Fritzella dealt the cards in a careful pattern upon a small table. There appeared to be a sort of cross in the center, and a vertical line of four cards at the right.

The older woman studied the arrangement carefully, glancing up at Marianne from time to time. The girl felt a shiver run through her, as if she were in the presence of something she did not understand. What did these cards say of her? She wondered if they could truly see what was in her future.

"Now you must ask me a question," said Fritzella. "It must be on a point of keen interest to you, and it must be one that can be answered with a simple yes or no. This will help to guide my impressions into the proper channels.''

''That's not difficult!'' Marianne said, feeling relieved. ''My question is, will my plan with Lord Whitestone succeed?''

Again the silence lengthened in the room. Miss Crane closed her eyes, and from her expression her thoughts appeared to be far away. Marianne speculated about whether she had really lived before and could remember it, and decided that at least the old woman believed it to be true. It seemed so odd, so un-Christian, and yet Miss Crane was the soul of propriety; the Sloans would not have entrusted Marianne to her care otherwise.

She tried to imagine what it would be like to have been a slave girl in Greece, or a peasant girl in France six centuries ago, but all she could think of were flat pictures, like scenes from old paintings.

At last the other woman spoke. ''There is someone watching you from afar,'' she said. ''Someone who is very concerned for your welfare.''

''Grandfather?''

''I do not think so,'' said Miss Crane. ''Farther away than that, I should think.''

''Go on,'' Marianne urged.

''There are many forces at work here,'' said Miss Crane. ''This is a most unusual fortune. So many things, it is difficult to sort them out.''

Marianne forced herself to sit silent so Fritzella could concentrate. Surely her life was not really so complex as all that.

''There is a man also,'' she said. ''I see him surrounded by many women. But you stand apart from them. However, the outcome is not clear. Perhaps you stand apart because you are special to him, or perhaps you are only excluded from the company.''

''That sounds more likely,'' Marianne conceded.

''There is a woman who could harm you. You should be very cautious with her. She is standing near the man.''

''Serena Brinoli!'' said Marianne. The other woman looked startled.

''How do you know of her?''

"I saw her today in the jewellery store," said Marianne. "But surely she could not really resent me. A woman in her position cannot truly expect that a marquis would wed her."

"Let me tell you a lesson learned over many centuries," said Miss Crane. "What a woman ought to expect, and what she does expect, are not always the same thing, especially where a man is concerned."

"Is there anything else in the cards?"

"Yes, but it is too confusing," said Fritzella, throwing up her hands. "It could be read a thousand ways, and none of them correct. We shall simply have to proceed as best we can."

"When shall we go to Vauxhall? Tomorrow night?"

Miss Crane frowned thoughtfully. "We shall see. The time must be right."

4

"YOU ARE COMMITTING a grave error." Sir Edward Beamish propped one Hussar-booted foot on the small table as he lounged back in his chair in his friend's dressing room. "Do you think Serena Brinoli wants for admirers? Do you think she will pine for you?"

"I most sincerely hope not." Jeremy Hanbridge, Marquis of Whitestone, examined his cravat in the looking glass. It was most excellently done up in the elaborate Trone d'Amour style. "Why do we submit to these contortions with our neckcloths?"

"I prefer it to the powdered wigs our fathers wore, don't you?" observed his friend, sipping on a glass of brandy.

The marquis took a last look at his plum-coloured coat of superfine and his dove-grey, close-fitting breeches. "Shall we go?"

"Even Beau Brummel himself would approve," Ned Beamish agreed, rising abruptly and swallowing the last of his brandy. "But Serena will pay scant attention to your appearance when you give her the news."

"She has no grounds for complaint," said Jeremy as they descended the marquis's main staircase together. "Only last week I gave her a ruby necklace to match her earrings, and the lease on the house is paid for another three months. She will have found another patron long before that."

Jeremy would have preferred to take his phaeton, a dashing vehicle the colour of bronze, but it seated only two, and there would be four of them. Instead, the two men took seats inside the carriage, with its brushed-brass hardware and brown velvet squabs, and allowed the coachman to pilot the way to Serena's house to collect their ladyloves.

"Perhaps Serena will not be unduly perturbed, but I am," Ned admitted at last as they jounced over the streets of London.

"You?" Jeremy looked at him in surprise. "Why should you care that I relinquish my mistress?"

"Were you merely to change mistresses, I should not care," said his friend. "But although you refuse to speak of it, I cannot escape the conclusion that you are contemplating matrimony."

"Nothing of the sort."

"You concede you have behaved queerly since your little jaunt into the country?" Ned peered at him but received no response. "Priscilla Land and Lucinda Marlow are as keen on you as ever, but I do not think it is one of them. You are not enamoured of some country mouse?"

"You refine on this too much," said Jeremy. "Let us speak of other matters."

"Very well." Ned settled back. "There is a bet at White's that Marlow is going to call you out."

"What, that old man? Don't believe a word of it."

"Not the earl. Lord Charles."

Jeremy's mouth hardened into a thin line. "Let the whole bloody lot of them challenge me to duel at once, I shall never change my mind."

"No one's disagreeing with you," said Ned quickly, having learned over the years the ill effects of arguing with Jeremy Hanbridge when he became fixed in a matter. Fortunately, the marquis was normally of equable temperament and not easily roused. "One can see that so long as the chit protects that traitor of a father—"

"Precisely." Jeremy continued staring out the window as the carriage came to a halt.

Serena Brinoli and Libby Holcomb allowed themselves to be handed into the carriage with dispatch. Both were exquisitely gowned and wrapped in shawls against the chill, for one must travel by water to Vauxhall if one were to enjoy the magic of it fully.

"A splendid evening, is it not?" Serena fingered her new ruby necklace. "Thank you, my lord, for your kind gift."

36

"It was nothing," said Lord Whitestone distantly. Serena frowned.

Libby Holcomb quickly filled in the gaps in the conversation with chatter, carefully watching to be sure she offended no one. She was a fetching thing, although with hair of an unnatural yellow. Not in Serena's class for looks, thought Ned, wondering idly how Whitestone would react if he took that man's castoff mistress for his own.

But he would not do that, Ned thought, giving himself a mental shake, for she came too dear. He did not even keep Libby. He preferred an occasional outing with a lightskirt, rewarding the woman with little gifts, to setting one up in housekeeping.

Freedom, that was the word for it. How fortunate that there were women in the world with the proper attitude, Ned reflected. He knew that his own medium colouring and slender build paled before the dashing good looks of his closest friend, but he had near eight thousand pounds a year and a title, and was not without his own personal charms.

As a result, he had been besieged by eager mamas, from ambitious cits hoping to raise their heiress daughters to the peerage, to ladies hanging out for a title for their offspring.

But the truth was, Ned Beamish could not abide well brought up young ladies. Had he a taste for the vivacious type of woman, he might have found one to suit, but he preferred a lass with an air of uncertainty, even a touch of naiveté. Yet underneath she must possess the spirit to respond to his lovemaking in kind, and he had found that properly demure young women turned to mush before his advances, like a cake left out in the rain.

I shall never marry, thought Ned with satisfaction. And bless me if I won't do my best to keep Jeremy from getting ensnarled.

That gentleman's thoughts, had Ned but known it, were already very much ensnarled. Despite his resolve to be gracious to Serena all evening before breaking the news to her, Jeremy found himself unable to carry on a conversation. His thoughts kept returning to the Hounsleys' garden and the mysterious slip of a girl he had met there.

Who was she? Where had she come from, and why had she vanished so suddenly? He had never met anyone like her before, had never imagined a woman could be so desirable and companionable and provocative and comfortable, all at once.

In her presence, Jeremy had found himself stirred both physically and emotionally, tantalised in a way that had spoiled him forever for Serena's artifices. Perhaps it was the romantic setting, he tried to tell himself, but then, had he not seen other women in gardens?

She had gone as suddenly and untraceably as she had come. While the marquis had not wished to create gossip by searching too openly, he had made discreet inquiries at the ball, but no one had recalled seeing a young woman of that description. Nor had he spotted her the next day among the guests who were staying with the Hounsleys, and it seemed unlikely one of the neighbours who had come by carriage would have departed so early.

He was roused from his thoughts as the group alighted at Westminster and took a gaily beribboned barge to Spring Gardens, Vauxhall. Jeremy stirred himself to make polite conversation, then lapsed into his reverie again as the lamps from the barge sent ripples of light shivering over the water.

Could she truly have been a creature of magic, a faery? It was preposterous, surely. She had been only jesting when she said she might appear anywhere, at any time.

What made the matter even more frustrating was that Jeremy could not vent his concerns in the usual manner, by writing to his secret correspondent, the insightful and clever Mata. Somehow he felt free to divulge to her, in anonymous letters, what he never would have dared tell anyone he knew. Yet now she was gone —but where?

He had tried over these past months to ascertain her identity, but the editors at the *Gazette* steadfastly honoured her request for secrecy. Frustrated, Jeremy tried to visualise her, and decided she must be an old maid, a talented and deeply sensitive woman who had perhaps lost her fiancé in the war, or had been abandoned by some unfeeling cad.

Although he had been curious to meet her, in a way Jeremy felt relieved that Mata had not come to London. In fact, he suspected that her supposed sudden absence from home was but an excuse for her not to come. No doubt she herself realised that once the two met, they could never again be so easy and open in their correspondence. At any rate, he resolved to write to her of his dilemma and hope that she would respond.

"You are uncommon quiet tonight, my lord," murmured Serena. "Have I displeased you?"

He managed a smile. "Not at all. You are exquisite tonight, my dear." The words were true, but he felt hollow as he said them.

Serena hesitated. She could feel her grip on the marquis weakening, and she was uncertain how to proceed. She had no intention of overplaying her hand, not when there was such a large prize at stake. For while his lordship was handsome indeed, that was not the chief point of interest for Serena. She had clawed her way out of the gutter, had become through sheer force of will the elegant and refined creature she now appeared. But she was determined that this wouldn't be as far as she would reach, being mistress to a lord, easily cast off if he tired of her.

No, Serena thought, fingering the rubies at her neck. She would have a wedding ring, and a title, and the arrogant misses who gawked at her in shops and then turned away would have to call her "my lady," and curtsy as she went by. She would have jewels, and silk sheets, and half a dozen carriages. She would be the Marchioness of Whitestone.

Serena was gratified when they landed amid the enchanted lights of Vauxhall. Here she might reweave her web, in its wandering paths where a couple might lose themselves, even find a quiet place to make love in the moonlight. She must bind this man to her, win him to propose in a moment of weakness or jealousy. He must be hers.

Yet as she slipped her arm through his, Serena had to admit to herself that she would never have been invited to accompany his lordship to a ball. Even at the opera she had her own box, where he might visit her. That was discreet, but she knew he would never actually take her to a performance.

Vauxhall, however, was open to anyone for the price of three shillings sixpence. Ruffians and footpads prowled here, and women of easy virtue that any man might have for a few shillings, as well as elegant ladies and gentlemen, and families of the middle class. All came to hear the concerts at the rotunda, and partake of a cold collation and, in some cases, seek flirtation and perhaps a lovers' rendezvous among the twelve acres of hedges, trees, pavillions, temples, pillars, statues and cascades.

The small party approached the rotunda and found a table where they might enjoy a supper and listen to the orchestra. Serena tried not to let Lord Whitestone see that she observed him glancing about, as if absentmindedly seeking someone.

Ned was looking about at the ladies also, but that was his manner. Libby, a timid little milk-and-water miss, merely stared with widened eyes at the brilliant assemblage, the ladies in their silken gowns and the gentlemen in their evening finery. That chit would never be able to promote her own interest, Serena reflected.

Then she experienced a surge of irritation at espying a party settling down at a table not far off. She had never been introduced to Lucinda Marlow, of course, but had seen her at the opera once, and knew her to be one of those who had set her cap for Lord Whitestone.

Pinch-faced thing, Serena thought. Surely he cannot be looking for her!

She indulged in a careful study of Lucinda and her party. There was a mousy girl—she must be Lucinda's younger sister, Jane, just coming out this season, who looked as if a sharp word might destroy her entirely. The formidable older man was surely their father, Lord Charles, and the equally formidable woman their mother.

It was too bad they had not brought that traitor's daughter, Miss Arnet, with them. That would be an evening's entertainment, to see them snubbed by Lord Whitestone.

"Excuse me," Jeremy said, standing up. "I must convey my greetings." He walked toward the Marlow table.

"I fear I must, too," said Sir Edward.

"It surprises me that Lord Whitestone would be welcomed by them, when one considers how he has insulted their family," Serena said.

Ned smiled. "Ah, but this is polite society, and we are unfailingly polite, if never terribly sincere." He followed his friend.

Serena tapped her fan on the table in annoyance. "Someday I will be introduced to them, and they will be polite to me as well," she said.

"Oh, but surely that cannot be," gasped Libby. "They would never greet one of us. We are beyond the pale."

"There have been instances where lords have taken their mistresses for their wives."

"Do you really think Lord Whitestone might?" The chit was positively astounded, as if such a thing had never occurred to her.

"I declare, you have more hair than brains!" Serena snapped. "Do you think I will be satisfied with mere baubles?"

"If only one could know for sure what will be," Libby sighed.

"One can, my ladies, and for only five shillings," said a girl's voice nearby, startling them both.

"Where did you come from?" Serena turned to stare into the face of a gypsy girl, her hair tied back under a kerchief, her skirts multicoloured and ragged. "You have a familiar look about you. Have we met before?"

"Perhaps in a previous existence," said the girl. "The past is full of such mysteries. But the future need not be. For only five shillings, Madame Cransky will tell your fortune with the ancient Tarot, and reveal all to you. I do assure you, she is quite expert."

"Your accent comes and goes," Serena sniffed and saw the girl flush. "I do not believe you are a gypsy at all. You are a fraud. You will lure us into the bushes and your brother will attack and rob us."

"That is not true," said the girl earnestly. "You are quite right that I am not a gypsy, but Madame Cransky is, and she needed an assistant, and I did need a place so badly. We shall wait until the gentlemen return, and they will come along and see that you are safe."

Serena hesitated. She did not care to have her fortune told, especially in the presence of Lord Whitestone, unless . . .

"This Madame Cransky," she said. "There are certain things I might wish to have said in the presence of this particular gentleman. Do you think, if I were to pay her two shillings extra, she would oblige me?"

The girl hesitated. "I will have to ask," she said finally. "I will return in just a moment."

"Wait." Serena held up her hand. "By then the gentlemen may have returned. What I wish said is that I have been a great lady in . . . in a previous existence, and that I was born to be one again in this."

"I will ask her." The girl slipped away into the darkness.

"How exciting!" cried Libby. "I've never had my fortune told! Do you think she can really see the future?"

"Vauxhall is full of charlatans and thieves," said Serena calmly. "I would put no more faith in what some old crone tells me from a deck of cards than I would in curses uttered by a street urchin. But it will provide us with amusement, and perhaps distract our friends from the other pleasures to be found here this evening."

Lord Whitestone was not at that moment very pleased. He was feeling a distinct chill emanating from the person of The Honourable Charles Marlow, much to the distress of Mrs. and Miss Marlow, who were fluttering about and making a fuss over their visitor.

"We do hope to see you at Jane's come-out ball next week," said Mrs. Marlow. "Lord and Lady Sefton have already replied in the affirmative and the Princess Esterhazy has indicated she will attend also."

Jeremy hesitated. He did not wish to commit himself to a dull evening with a gaggle of silly young girls. The joys of come-out balls had faded this past year or so, now that he had reached the advanced age of thirty. Yet, he reminded himself, he must cast aside his instinct to remain solitary, for only by attending all manner of festivities could he hope to encounter again his mysterious young lady, if indeed she had come to London.

"Naturally, I shall be charmed to attend," he said.

"Will you be coming too?" the timid younger sister asked, looking up wide-eyed at Ned.

Jeremy could see his friend swallow quickly. This girl was very much to the baronet's taste, shy and demure, but no doubt she would remain so under all circumstances, which would *not* be to the baronet's taste. Knowing Ned's dislike of matchmaking mamas, who were ever so abundant at these affairs, Jeremy decided to bedevil his friend in return for being remarkably unsympathetic to his own wish to give up Serena.

"I believe I can speak for Sir Edward when I say he has been looking forward to nothing more, and will certainly be attending with me," Jeremy intoned, and bit his lip to keep from smiling.

Lucinda toyed with a lock of her chestnut hair as she gazed obliquely up at the marquis. "We are so glad you have decided not to hold certain matters against us. One can hardly help one's family relations, you know."

"Lucinda!" Jane slapped one hand on the table in outrage. "How dare you? Our cousin is as dear to us—"

"I believe this conversation is best avoided," said Mrs. Marlow quickly. Noticing the thunderclouds gathering in her husband's face, Jeremy made a hasty departure.

"Did you notice how that little chit lit into Lucinda?" said Ned admiringly as they strolled back across the lawn. "One wouldn't expect it of her."

"It is unfortunate that her loyalty is misplaced," said Jeremy, then added conciliatingly, "I suppose it would be unnatural of her to despise her own cousin, whom she surely knew before Arnet's treachery was revealed."

"Lucinda, it would appear, is the unnatural one," observed Ned. "It is not she you are thinking of wedding, is it?"

"I am not planning to marry anyone." Jeremy lowered his voice as they approached the table where Serena and Libby sat.

"We are going to have our fortunes told!" cried Libby, jumping up. "Do say we may!" She looked pleadingly at the baronet. "It is only five shillings, and I have never had mine read before!"

"What a bunch of folderol," snorted Ned. "Fortunes told? It is all trickery and deceit, and none of it ever comes true."

Jeremy looked at Serena. It was not like her to agree to such lower-class nonsense. "What do you think of it, my dear?"

She cocked her head to one side as if deep in thought. "It is this way, my lord. I have made certain inquiries which, if they are answered to my satisfaction, would indicate that this old gypsy woman may have some merit. Her assistant has gone to put the matter to her, and should return shortly. Ah, there she is."

A slim figure in colourful garb darted forward from the

shadows. Jeremy could see little of her as she stood talking quietly to Serena, her back to him.

Serena was nodding. "She meets with my approval, my lord. Shall we go?"

"Very well." He offered her his arm, and the foursome set out to follow the scampering gypsy girl.

Lucinda pouted as she watched them go. "It is all your fault, Jane," she snapped. "You have driven them away! Now Lord Whitestone will not attend our ball, and he will never look at me again!"

"Better he does not!" cried Jane. "He is not worthy to be a member of this family."

"I agree," said their father. "I am not entirely sure that were he to offer for Lucinda, I should not send him packing."

"Charles! You cannot be serious!" exclaimed his wife.

This domestic scene resolved itself rapidly as two other gentlemen of their acquaintance approached. One, the Honourable Horace Trimble, the pear-shaped and exceedingly vain younger son of a viscount, held a post in the Foreign Office. The other, his cousin, Mr. Frederick Falmby, was an impoverished member of the untitled gentry and destined for the clergy.

"Ladies! How exquisite you are looking." Mr. Trimble, wearing yellow pantaloons, a lavender waistcoat and a coat of scarlet velvet, swept them a garish bow. His companion, sedately clad in dark blue, nodded politely.

Inspiration swept over Lucinda. "Oh, Father, I saw a gypsy girl just now, and some ladies following her. I am sure they went to have their fortunes told." Her father, apparently, had not noticed that Lord Whitestone had been with them, and she hoped to encounter him again, without her disapproving family. "Please may I go? I am sure these gentlemen would escort me, would you not?"

"We would be overwhelmed with pleasure," said Mr. Trimble. "Fortunes told, is it? Perhaps if she has some good to say of me, I could present her to my creditors, who might be kept at bay a while longer on the strength of it."

"Of course they shall go, shan't they?" their mother urged. "And Jane as well. It is harmless business, and most entertaining." Clearly she had grasped Lucinda's plan, her daughter thought with satisfaction.

"Do you think it wise, madame?" asked Mr. Falmby earnestly. "As a future member of the clergy, I feel obliged to point out that it is through such frivolities that young ladies may be led into error."

"Do you truly think so?" Jane inquired. "It seems harmless enough to me."

"Indeed, he does not think so," sniffed Lucinda. "It is merely that he feels it incumbent upon himself, as a young and inexperienced person, to impress us with his gravity and moral rectitude. Well, it is all pomposity, that is what it is, and I shall not be swayed by it."

Without waiting for her father's permission, she swept away, with Mr. Trimble huffing to keep up. After a moment's hesitation, Mr. Falmby offered Jane a stiff arm and they set off sedately behind the other pair.

"Lucinda has been insufferable tonight," Jane said. "I do beg your pardon, Mr. Falmby, that she should address you in this manner. When she is in ill humour, which fortunately is not often, she shares her ill temper most generously with the rest of us."

"I think you are harsh on your sister," replied her companion. "Upon reflection, I fear I spoke out of turn."

They walked in silence down a gravel walk between high hedges, until they reached the other couple in a small grove.

"There is someone here before us," Lucinda said gaily, turning to meet them. "Imagine that! I never knew having one's fortune told was all the crack, but it seems to be tonight."

Jane glanced into the grove. "Why, that is Lord Whitestone and Sir Edward." Then she stopped in horror. "Those women! Look at that yellow hair! They're lightskirts!"

"We shall be off at once," said Mr. Falmby, shocked.

"You be off!" cried Lucinda. "Do you think we shall have our fun spoiled by your missish ways? Fie on you!" And she smacked his arm with her fan.

"Shame on you, sister!" said Jane. "You behave little better than a lightskirt yourself tonight. I shall be happy to return with Mr. Falmby."

But that gentleman was staring at Lucinda in amazement. "You struck me," he said.

"And I shall strike you again!" She rapped his arm once more. "There! Have you become accustomed to it?"

"I shall die of humiliation," Jane wailed.

"I say, is it my imagination or is it rather damp this evening?" inquired Mr. Trimble, who had been paying no attention. "Do you think the crease is coming out of my neckcloth?"

"Oh, pooh on your cravat, you great gawk!" Jane, her temper frayed, swatted him over the head with her own fan, breaking its ribs.

"The entire world has gone mad," said Mr. Falmby with a touch of admiration.

"Are these rogues distressing you, ladies?" Jane looked up and saw to her consternation that the voice belonged to Sir Edward Beamish.

"I . . ." The dangling wreck of her fan caught her eye. "Oh, dear, I fear we must all seem to be a trifle foxed."

"Would anyone else care to have her fortune—" The gypsy girl stopped suddenly as she emerged from among the trees. Jane took one look, then stumbled backwards and fell to the ground in a faint.

= 5 =

THE EVENING HAD gone surprisingly well for Marianne and Miss
Crane. They had learned that many members of the ton would be
at Vauxhall that night for an exceptionally fine concert; even the
Marlows were going, Celia had said. So they decided to make their
move.

Fritzella's closets proved a treasure trove of paraphernalia. There
were costumes for the two of them, a little canopy that unfolded
on four poles and could be erected to create a bit of privacy, and
stools and a small folding table.

A footman had come along with them on the barge, at Will's
insistence, and aided in arranging their little gypsy encampment.
He had also been duly instructed to keep a watchful eye on
Marianne as she flitted about seeking the proper party, for in the
vastness of Vauxhall, a young girl alone might at any moment find
herself swept off by a villain to be ravished in the bushes.

The gypsy ladies had practiced their arts on several patrons
before locating the marquis, and had received considerable ac-
claim. Fritzella was indeed talented, or else a very shrewd student
of human nature, Marianne reflected.

She had been intimidated at first to see Whitestone in the company of his paramour, but reproached herself for her timidity. She
could hardly expect that one encounter with her in a garden at the
Hounsleys' would have made much of an impression, certainly not
enough to cause him to cast off his mistress and pine of unrequited
love.

Serena had been won over with surprising ease, and Marianne

had managed to keep the marquis, who might have given the game away most embarrassingly, from spotting her at first. Serena was quickly manoeuvred into the little canopy.

At her insistence, the marquis stood nearby to hear her fortune, looking quite bored with the proceedings. Miss Crane gave him a sly look before she began to lay out the cards.

Marianne found herself waiting impatiently. What would Fritzella say, and how would it affect the two listeners? She wished she knew how Whitestone really felt about his trollop.

"I see a great lady," intoned the ersatz Madame Cransky. "A great lady from a former existence, who has come amongst us again."

Serena nodded happily.

"I see also many men—let me count them—three, four—"

Serena's expression changed into a stormy frown. "I fear you are mistaken, madame."

"Of course these refer to father and brothers, do they not?" asked Miss Crane with feigned innocence. "I cannot understand why this should distress you."

"Indeed, it does not," sniffed Serena.

Marianne, who had kept her face carefully averted, could not resist a sidelong look at the marquis. He was trying unsuccessfully to repress a smile, until his glance caught hers and he registered amazement.

"I see a great lady in this existence as well," Miss Crane was saying. "She is surrounded by admirers. Yes, there is much richness here, many jewels—"

"I am sure you are boring Lord Whitestone," said Serena quickly.

"Yes," his lordship said distractedly. "Yes, perhaps I should step outside." He nodded urgently to Marianne over Serena's head, and she followed discreetly as Miss Crane droned on. Marianne had a feeling this was going to be a very lengthy fortune.

"By Jove, it is you!" Lord Whitestone exclaimed when they were alone. "What is this gypsy garb? Who are you?"

Gazing up into his dark, compelling eyes, Marianne was finding it suddenly very difficult to maintain her pretence. Only the memory of what would happen if she revealed her true identity enabled her to retain her composure.

"Did I not say I might appear anywhere, at any time?" she asked. "Tonight I have chosen to be a gypsy girl."

"I don't understand." The tall, handsome man before her wore a look of confusion that matched his words. "No lady would be allowed to run about Vauxhall dressed as you are, yet no ragamuffin would have been invited to the Hounsleys'."

"Then it must be that I am neither a lady nor a ragamuffin," said Marianne, wishing her breathing would return to normal.

"You must have a name, at least."

"I have," she said. "In fact, I have a dozen names."

His expression darkened. "You are toying with me."

Marianne sighed. "It is not that I wish to, my lord. I fear if you knew who I really am, you would scorn me."

"Never," he said.

"I may not reveal my true name, for there are others who might be harmed," she went on. "If I adopt disguises, if I seem to trick you, it is only that I wish to be your friend, and I may only be that by behaving as I do."

"Do you mean you have come here to Vauxhall tonight, dressed in this manner, solely for the purpose of meeting me?" he asked in astonishment.

Marianne nodded. "Yes, my lord."

"Do you know who I am?"

"Lord Whitestone," she said.

"Did you know the first time we met?"

She shook her head. "I was not attempting to deceive you then. But now that I know the difference between us—"

"Nonsense." The marquis thrust his chin forward determinedly. "No one may come between us if we do not wish it. Does someone threaten you? I assure you, I will not tolerate it."

"The person who threatens me has no fear of you," Marianne said. "Indeed, I believe he could easily overpower you, although not in the manner you may be thinking. Please, let us talk no more of identities or fears. We have so few minutes together."

"But this is intolerable." Jeremy stared at her in frustration.

Then the look in his eyes softened. "Please say I may see you again." He reached forward, gently gripping her shoulders.

Marianne felt herself trembling at his touch, and longed for him to pull her close. "You may see me again," she whispered. "As often as I may contrive."

He pulled her closer, and her eyelids seemed to half-shut of their own accord, and her face tilted upwards toward him as their lips met, gently, urgently.

Her arms wound about his neck, and his about her waist, and they pressed against each other hungrily. A great ache filled Marianne, and a longing that only he could fill. She kissed him eagerly, and felt his hands stroke her back lovingly.

A weakness seeped through her, and Marianne leaned against him for support. At that moment, had he picked her up and carried her off, she would not have uttered so much as a murmur of protest.

"What is this?" At Serena's furious tone, the two sprang apart guiltily.

"It is what it appears," said Lord Whitestone calmly. "I make no explanations."

Serena turned her fury on Marianne. "Why, you little whore!" She stepped forward with her hand raised but Jeremy grabbed her wrist before she could strike.

"I have something to say to you in private, Serena," he snapped. "Pray excuse us, miss."

"Of course." Her cheeks burning, Marianne scurried back to the little canopy.

She peered inside and saw that Libby was seated at the table. Marianne hesitated. She wanted desperately to rush back to Lord Whitestone, to hold him again and feel his breath mingle with hers, but she knew she must not. For one thing, he was clearly having an angry discussion with his mistress. Furthermore, she must not appear too willing, too easily conquered, although how she was to resist his overwhelming presence in future, she could not imagine.

The sound of angry female voices and a slapping noise drew her attention to a nearby grove. As Marianne approached, she realised the people were most likely waiting their turn with Miss Crane.

Libby was rising, so Marianne hurried forward. "Would anyone else care to have her fortune—" She halted in surprise as her eyes met Jane's, and then watched in horror as her cousin sank to the ground in a faint.

"Jane!" cried Marianne, quite forgetting herself. She plunged down beside her cousin and began to slap her cheeks lightly. "Do wake up. It is not at all like you to faint in this manner."

"You would seem to be on uncommon familiar terms with this lady," said an amused male voice from overhead. Marianne glanced up. Oh, dear! This companion of Lord Whitestone's must certainly be Sir Edward Beamish, whom Lucinda had said was the marquis's closest friend. And now she had all but revealed herself before him!

It was Lucinda who came to the rescue. Clearly terrified that the marquis would discover the loathed Marianne Arnet here in London, she said, "My sister has the most unaccountable knack of befriending strays, all manner of riffraff. I suppose her shock was in seeing that this young person, whom she had thought safely in a post as a governess, has returned to the streets to ply her trade as a gypsy."

"Y-yes," Jane agreed, coming round, then addressing Marianne. "Good heavens, what *are* you doing here?"

"Come and have your fortune told," said Marianne. "I shall explain it then."

"May I come?" The baronet ignored the return of his yellow-haired companion and fixed his gaze on Jane. "I should like to know more about the younger Miss Marlow."

By now, Jane had recovered her presence of mind. "Our acquaintance is scarcely great enough to admit of your hearing the most intimate details of my future," she said.

"Unless I am to figure in it?" It was difficult to ascertain if he were in earnest.

"You are impertinent," said Jane, attempting to snap her fan shut and finding to her dismay that the thing merely scraped about limply. "Oh, dear. I struck someone with this, did I not?"

"A very odd occurrence indeed," said a pear-shaped gentleman who had been standing in the background. "I merely made a casual remark regarding my clothing—"

"In the presence of ladies?" said the baronet in mock horror. "It is no wonder the poor thing fainted."

"This is all becoming horribly muddled," said the man Marianne later learned was Mr. Trimble. "I say, Freddie, shall we go on about our business?"

"I shall stay and escort the ladies back," said his companion.

Marianne pulled Jane away, glad to let the others sort themselves out as best they could.

"Now tell me why you are here at Vauxhall dressed as a gypsy!" Jane demanded. "This is scandalous!"

"Oh, but it is all part of a wonderful plan," said Marianne. "Now come and meet Miss Fritzella Crane, who is masquerading as Madame Cransky."

The matter was quickly explained, in whispers. Jane was at first incredulous, but Miss Crane and the footman—who appeared in a timely manner—reassured her that her cousin was not truly exposed to any dangers.

"I shall assist you, if I can," Jane said at last. "Sir Edward Beamish seems rather taken with me, although I should not be at all interested in a gentleman who disports himself with a yellow-haired hussy. Still, I might encourage him so that I may learn more about the marquis."

"That would be capital!" cried Marianne. "Shall you be at Almack's Wednesday? Celia has just succeeded in procuring a voucher for me."

"Yes, it is my first time!" said Jane. "I am so glad you will be there. I have been awfully blue-devilled without you, Marianne. It makes me so angry! I am glad to be able to help in your revenge."

But as she listened to Miss Crane tell Jane's fortune, Marianne was no longer so certain she wanted revenge. What she wanted at the moment was to be held in Lord Whitestone's arms and teased and cherished. If only this business of her parents hadn't come between them!

According to the cards, Jane's future held much happiness, although not without a few contrarieties. At last Jane departed reluctantly to rejoin the others, and Marianne, not wishing to face Lucinda's sharp tongue, made good her own escape.

Espying a tall figure not far off, she made her way toward Lord Whitestone, who was now alone.

"I did not mean to cause you trouble," she said as she approached. "Had I realised your friend would see us—"

"It is no matter in the end," he said, a trifle wearily. "I had meant to tell her farewell this evening, although I had hoped in a less dramatic manner."

On closer examination, Marianne could see a red mark across his cheek, as if he had been slapped. "Where has she gone?"

"Stormed off." He shrugged. "The woman is capable of terrible rages, although this is the first time she has turned on me. I have no doubt I will find her at our table ready to be escorted home. She is no fool."

Marianne felt uncomfortable. She knew so little of relationships of this type between men and women, and regretted having involved herself in the midst of one. She feared she had caused Miss Brinoli much pain, which had not been her intention. Indeed, she had no hopes of her own where Lord Whitestone was concerned, whatever her heart might wish.

"You are a strange one." His lordship leaned one shoulder against a tree and studied her intensely. "Clearly you are a young woman of good breeding, and yet you show no shock at discovering my relationship with a demimondaine. Rather than flying into the boughs at having been exposed to her sharp tongue, you appear apologetic."

Marianne twisted her hands together. "I had thought this would be rather a lark, dressing up as a gypsy," she said. "But I hate deceit. It is foreign to me."

"Then abandon it."

"Will you believe me that I cannot? That otherwise I must never see you again?"

She heard him draw a breath sharply. "Tell me, are you married?" he said.

She shook her head. "No, it is not that, my lord."

"Then why can you not trust me enough to confide in me?" He stepped forward and grasped her shoulders lightly. "You have not even given me a name to call you by."

Marianne looked up at him and felt herself wanting to surrender. Surely he would not shun her now.

"I say, Jeremy?" Lord Whitestone swore under his breath and stepped away at the sound of Ned Beamish's voice. "Jeremy, where the deuce—ah, there you are!" The baronet sauntered toward them. "Oh, sorry to interrupt your little dalliance! I did not see the young lady."

"It is not a dalliance!" said Lord Whitestone stiffly. Marianne felt herself turning crimson.

"Indeed, indeed," said Sir Edward, looking not at all perturbed. "Damned strange goings-on. Serena just cut through in a huff and hauled Libby off with her. Near slapped my face when I tried to cry halt. See *your* face got a bit of the old dust-off, eh?"

"If this is what you've come to tell me—"

"No, no, knew I was forgetting something," the baronet said, apparently enjoying his friend's discomfiture. " 'Twas something that macaroni Trimble said. Was describing you as rather peculiar, don't you know, for being so set against this Miss Arnet. Everybody's heard about it, it seems."

Marianne's hand gripped the folds of her skirt tensely. What ill timing the man had!

"What of it, then?" demanded the marquis.

"Trimble says Priscilla Land heard from some friend of hers at the Hounsleys' that Miss Arnet was coming to London after all," said the baronet. "Odd turn, ain't it? Miss Jane turned all white and then red and told him to take his expanded waistline and parade it elsewhere. Those were her very words. Wouldn't expect it from a meek little thing like that, would you?"

"What about Miss Arnet?" Lord Whitestone said grimly.

"She's not with the Marlows, that's for certain," said his friend. "Lucinda came back from crossing the old woman's palm with gold, or what have you, and denied all of it. Then Miss Jane said their cousin could go wherever she pleased, and the two of them bloody near made a fight of it."

"You stopped them, I hope?" Marianne said, worried. If her visit to London were going to turn two sisters into enemies, perhaps she had better return to the countryside at once.

"No need," said their informant. "Mr. Falmby stepped in the

way and got roundly kicked by the elder Miss Marlow for his pains.
She won't apologise, either. Don't know what you see in that
woman, Jeremy. Now her younger sister is another story."

"It's no concern of mine whether the Misses Marlow pull each
other's hair out or not," snapped the marquis. "But what about
this rumour? Is there any truth in it?"

Ned shrugged. "Hard to say. Priscilla's a great one for gossip,
ain't she? Not all of it quite truthful. I expect the earl's been putting it about that he's not afraid of being snubbed by anybody.
Maybe she's coming to stay at an inn and do some shopping, just
to show her family won't bend the old knee to the great Marquis
of Whitestone."

"That had better be all there is to it." His lordship's eyes were
narrowed and he wore a look of hard, cold hatred that Marianne
had never seen in him before.

"But who is this Miss Arnet?" she ventured, hoping he
wouldn't hear the slight tremor in her voice. "Why should you
hate her so?"

"She is the daughter of a French traitor who's responsible for
the deaths of many of my men, and nearly for my own," said the
marquis.

"Surely she could hardly be held to blame—"

"I won't have you defending her!" To Marianne's surprise,
Lord Whitestone glared at her. "Not even you! Although I realise
you do so merely from a kind heart. It's clear she knows her
father's whereabouts and, further, I find it highly likely she passes
messages for him."

"Yet this is all guesswork, surely," Marianne ventured. "And
with Napoleon in retreat before our armies, perhaps it will soon
come out that she's quite innocent."

"You do not know these people," Lord Whitestone said. "Furthermore, she would be an unnatural child, would she not, were
she to disown her parents and refuse them aid?"

"It seems the poor girl is trapped, then," said Marianne.
"Either she must be unnatural by abandoning her parents, or a
traitor, which is surely unnatural as well."

The marquis's expression softened. "I have never met a woman
who reasoned as cleverly as you, my dear. With you to argue her

case, perhaps even Miss Arnet might be acquitted by a jury of her peers. But not by me. Unlike you, I have seen the devastation of treachery at first hand. I shall never be induced to consider her anything but a shame to this country, only slightly less so than her parents.''

The baronet changed the conversation then, and Marianne tried to swallow the dark, nasty feeling in her throat. For a moment, the marquis had even turned on her, merely for defending Miss Arnet. If he ever found out that she was indeed that person, there would be no more friendship between them.

Yet she would not retreat! She would not run off to the country and hide, as if she were guilty of something. Marianne felt her head come up proudly. Even if it broke her heart, she would establish herself here, win the marquis to her. Although she must then lose him, by that time all London would know of their romance, and it would be he who would retreat to the country in embarrassment.

''Shouldn't you gentlemen like to have your fortunes told?'' she asked with renewed resolve.

''Anything to please you,'' said the marquis gallantly, although the baronet declined, saying he had best hasten back to help escort the Misses Marlow to their parents. A weak sop like Mr. Falmby could hardly be trusted to extend adequate protection to the eminently protectable Miss Jane.

Madame Cransky laid the cards for the marquis carefully. ''You have no faith in my abilities,'' she told him, a fact that was evident from the way he sat atop his stool with arms folded skeptically. ''For most gentlemen, I would not waste my time with such an attitude. However, I shall make an exception.''

''Most kind of you,'' said the marquis drily.

''I see a great deal of pride,'' Miss Crane told him, studying the cards. ''Also much loyalty and honour, and honesty, and a sense of righteousness.''

Marianne realised she had been holding her breath, and tried to relax. Was Fritzella really reading the cards, or merely telling him what she already knew?

''Pray continue,'' said Lord Whitestone.

''Your cards show a number of women,'' said Miss Crane.

"Any one in particular?" He leaned forward, interested at last.

"Yes, but she is hidden," Fritzella said. "You cannot see her clearly, for you are blinded."

Marianne prayed silently that her friend was not so carried off by her own work that she would reveal too much. The marquis's response to the baronet minutes before had shown her only too clearly how hopeless the matter was.

"I am blinded?" Lord Whitestone repeated. "Do you not mean that I am blinded by her refusal to reveal herself?"

Miss Crane shook her head. "The key lies inside yourself. But of course there are many other ladies here, and they are clear to see. You may have your pick of them."

The marquis started to speak and then caught himself. "Is that all you see?"

Fritzella frowned. "There is something else here, something I believe I have seen before in another fortune. But it is difficult to decipher."

Lord Whitestone watched her intently. "What manner of thing?"

"Someone far away is watching you," said Miss Crane. "I cannot read whether this be friend or foe. But this person is in grave danger. It is possible that through you . . . but not directly through you . . . no, it is all confused now." She pressed her hand to her forehead.

Marianne moved forward quickly. "Are you ill, madame?" she asked. "Perhaps we had best go."

"Allow me to assist you," said the marquis. "I have a carriage waiting and would be happy to escort you."

Marianne hesitated. She had no wish to let the marquis see where she lived—indeed, it might spoil much of her plan—yet she could not sacrifice Fritzella's health.

However, just then the footman made his presence known, and assured his lordship that their own carriage should be awaiting them at this hour.

"Very well," the marquis said reluctantly, turning to Marianne. "I shall bid you good night."

He kissed her hand, looked deep into her eyes for one suspended moment, and then strode away into the night.

=6=

THE LETTER FROM J. arrived at the *Gazette* offices the next day, and as Will had gone to deliver a new poem of Marianne's, he fetched it home straight away. She took it to her room as soon as she could politely excuse herself.

"My dear Mata," she read, her hand trembling so that the paper quivered. "Although you have written that you will be absent, I find I have taken the habit of putting down my thoughts in letters to you, and so finding some measure of relief when I am perturbed."

Marianne sat on the edge of the bed, torn between dismay at learning that he was distressed and pleasure that he had written.

"Some curious events have transpired that seem, in the light of day, almost to have been imagined," the letter continued. "I have met a young woman who, unique among all my acquaintance, reminds me in her speech and manner of you."

Marianne looked up, her thoughts racing. Did he suspect she was Mata? If he did, that would not hint at her real identity, yet the possibility made her uncomfortable all the same. If Lord Whitestone's powers of perception were that keen, he might also see through her game. And if he discovered her before his romantic inclination became commonly known, she and her family might still be subject to ostracism. Drat him! she thought. If only he weren't so unjust, so priggishly self-righteous!

She read on as Whitestone described their two encounters and the strangeness of the mysterious woman's conduct. He begged Mata for her observations and advice as to how to proceed.

Part of Marianne wanted to reassure him. Oddly, she found no pleasure in the knowledge that his affections were becoming attached to her, since she could never receive them as Marianne Arnet. Instead, she felt pain at inflicting pain, and resolved not to write back. She could not stop him corresponding, nor herself reading what he wrote, but she would not encourage him to send his confidences to one who must be his enemy. At least, when he loathed and reviled her for having tricked him, he could not say she wilfully gave him any more hurt than necessary.

Oh, you fool! she told herself, folding the letter into a drawer. He will hardly make such nice distinctions.

She let herself, just for a moment, imagine that his feelings for her would be great enough to override his hatred of the Arnets. But in false hope lay only hopelessness for her future.

Resolutely, Marianne began to dress. She had been invited to join the Sloans at a small dinner party, after which there were to be more guests for cards. It was not to be a great literary encounter such as one might expect at Holland House, frequented as that was by Byron, Sheridan, and such wits as Henry Luttrell and J.P. Curran. Rather, Will had said, one might meet less established intellectuals, some writers and artists, and others of the nobility with a taste for clever conversation.

She selected a lilac jaconet muslin with a Greek-key pattern embroidered at the hem, and lilac ribbons for her blond hair. Marianne stared into the mirror thoughtfully as Rachel, who had come at her bidding, arranged her curls.

She tried to look critically at herself. The green eyes were unusual enough, but her face had none of the classic arrogance of Serena Brinoli's, nor the vivid colouring of Lucinda's, nor the distinction of Priscilla's.

He could not really care for her, Marianne told herself as Rachel tugged at a recalcitrant lock. He was merely fascinated by her manner of turning up in odd places, and her sauciness. What would he say when they met in polite society? Surely he would find her tedious then; he. . . . Oh, why must she think of him all the time? There were other men in the world, and someday she must learn to love one of them, for she could not have him.

The thought distressed her, and she was glad when she was able to escape downstairs. Miss Crane was out that evening, gone on one of her enigmatic errands. Marianne had asked where she went, but Fritzella said mildly that the matter was private.

Will and Celia smiled approvingly when they saw Marianne's costume. "We selected well, didn't we?" Celia asked her husband. "She is quite dashing. A diamond of the first water."

"A diamond in hot water, if anyone finds out who I am," Marianne said glumly.

"Oh, chin up," said Will. "It's all rather a lark, I think. That Lord Whitestone deserves a set-down."

"You had best not tell Lucinda of your plan," Celia warned. "I had tea with Edith today and she seems to believe Lord Whitestone is still a serious suitor, although from what you have told me, he cannot be."

"I did tell Jane, you know," Marianne said. "My head is whirling with it all. Shall we be off? I am looking forward to an evening where I can talk about serious matters, art and literature."

"Love is a serious matter also," said Celia as they went out.

The dinner party at the home of Will and Celia's friends, Henry and Marguerite Jones, proved as diverting as Marianne could have wished. With the trout Provençale, there was a discussion on Charles Lamb's essay on Shakespeare, and a lively debate as to whether indeed the subtlety of characterisation in the bard's work rendered the plays better fitted for reading than for performance. It mattered not to Marianne whether in fact Shakespeare should be acted or read; it was the quality of the discussion that enlivened her, for there were arguments of equal perspicacity on either side.

On the serving of the roast pork and tomatoes with sauce Hollandaise, the talk veered to the need for artists to find patrons. A lively debate ensued as to whether this necessity corrupted many artists of promise into portraiture or dull academic painting. It was decided, rather in jest, that a dedicated artist ought not to marry or have children, or else ought to be born rich.

By the time the creams were served and many glasses of port had been drunk, the conversation had grown ribald, with talk of the Italian custom of castrating young boys so that they would grow up to be male sopranos. Now that women were accepted on the stage, the cruel practice was dying out, but it was said that despite their rather grotesque appearance, the greatest of these castrati produced sounds of unearthly loveliness.

"After all," argued Will, "if all on stage is pretense, why may not a man pretend to be a woman?"

"Or a woman pretend to be a man?" answered Marianne.

"Your sister is right," said their host. "Perhaps it is time for a turnabout."

Marianne laughed. "Indeed. Provide me with suitable trousers and coat and I shall venture on the stage as Hamlet!" But she decided privately that appearing on the stage went a little beyond the lengths to which she was prepared to go in her enticement of Lord Whitestone.

At last, to her regret, the dinner ended and the other guests began to arrive to make up the card party. This was an end to the conversation Marianne had enjoyed so much.

She was also unpleasantly surprised to see both Priscilla Land and the future cleric, Mr. Frederick Falmby, among the arrivals. She determined to avoid them both, but this proved impossible, as Priscilla sought her out directly.

"We are all terribly curious, Miss Sloan," said Priscilla, as soon as they were introduced. "I understand you and your brother are distant cousins to the infamous Miss Arnet, and there is a rumour about that she has come to London."

"So I have heard," Marianne replied. "Although I believe the person who told me had heard this rumour from you."

Priscilla laughed lightly. "Very likely so. I am seen everywhere, you know. But you have a familiar air about you. Have we not met before?"

Marianne considered admitting to having been at the Hounsleys', but decided that to do so would be highly dangerous. On the other hand, suppose Priscilla later recalled having seen her there? This was all becoming so much more complicated than she had anticipated. She should have followed Lucinda's advice and avoided that ball altogether!

"I was briefly in London last year and perhaps we met then," she said, regretting the need for even a white lie.

"Tell me about Mademoiselle Arnet," said Priscilla. "Is she very pretty? Is she really a spy like her parents? And has she come to London?"

"As to whether she is pretty, she is well-enough looking but no beauty," said Marianne. "As for her being a spy, I am convinced she is not. And as to her being in London, what purpose would it serve if she did not go about in society? And if she did, you would surely hear of it."

"I shall trust you to tell me if she does come," said Priscilla with a feigned air of intimacy. "For Lucinda scarce speaks to me at all, since she knows Lord Whitestone prefers my company to hers, and Jane becomes quite violent when anyone speaks of her cousin, as if it were our fault she's a traitor."

"I have told you that is not the case," said Marianne sharply.

"Indeed, I had forgotten." Priscilla smiled sweetly. "I am sure if I had a cousin, I would think her incapable of evil as well." She moved off, leaving Marianne fuming.

Her ordeal was not over, however. She soon encountered Mr. Falmby, who also seemed to recall having met her before. It had been only the previous night, yet fortunately he did not connect the elegant young lady before him with the ragamuffin gypsy girl at Vauxhall.

"Everyone I meet seems to think we have been previously acquainted," said Marianne. "Miss Land said the very same thing to me. Perhaps there was some lady of a previous season who resembled me."

"No, I do not think that is it," said Mr. Falmby gravely. "However, I am pleased to make your acquaintance now. I am a great admirer of your cousin."

Marianne opened her mouth to say that Will was greatly liked everywhere, and remembered only just in time that he was not her cousin tonight but her brother. "My cousin?" she said carefully.

"Miss Lucinda Marlow," he said delicately, as if the name were an eggshell easily broken.

Marianne choked, then coughed into her gloved hand and spoke as easily as she could. "Oh, you are an admirer of my cousin. She is lovely, is she not?"

Mr. Falmby nodded sadly. "But I fear I have no chance with

her. I am only a poor younger son, and not a particularly handsome one at that."

"They say all things come to those who wait," Marianne advised. "It is difficult to say where Lucinda's eye may fall." Privately she doubted her cousin would ever feel affection for this timid young man, but she did not wish to crush his hopes, for one could never tell the future. Unless, perhaps, one were Madame Cransky.

Marianne found a pretext to slip away, and stood at the back of the room near the long gold draperies to avoid attracting notice.

She was glad she had chosen this spot when she saw who entered next: Lord Whitestone and Sir Edward Beamish.

Quickly catching Celia's eye, so that her cousin might make some explanation if her whereabouts were inquired after, Marianne slipped out the open floor-length windows.

However, she found the night air chilly on her bare arms and shoulders, for it was still only March, and so admitted herself through an unlocked side door. She found herself in the orangerie, a charming glass-walled room where potted orange trees and flowers bloomed.

Marianne discovered a small bench behind some of the trees and settled herself. The hour was close to half past ten, and she doubted that the two young bucks would choose to stay more than half an hour at such a sedate party. No doubt once they had played a few obligatory hands of whist, they would be off to livelier pursuits elsewhere.

Marianne amused herself by working on a poem in her mind. The picture that came to her was of a house, of doors and hallways and orangeries. Or perhaps a castle. Yes, a castle that was a metaphor for the world.

> The world is like a castle,
> Full of rooms and halls,
> Opening into windows,
> Closing into walls.

But the most interesting thing about a castle would be not the structure but the people who lived within, she thought, and added silently,

Some of us live in towers
Where sun and moonlight lie,
And some of us live on stairways
And watch the world go by.
But some of us are exiles, and
These beauties never know,
Because each craggy castle
Has dungeons down below.

She tried to imagine what it would be like, living in a dungeon.
It seemed unbearably grim.

And those who live in dungeons
May never see the sky,
Or touch the velvet curtains
Or watch the sparrows fly.

Marianne hesitated. She could not stop there; it was too melan-
choly. Yet what could a prisoner find to bring hope? Only, perhaps, the sound of his own inner voice.

But sometimes in the dungeon
Some hopeful voice will sing
To tell us that a castle
Must always have a king.

The first line, "The world is like a castle," would be her title,
and she would submit it to the *Gazette* the very next day, Marianne decided, pleased that her half hour in hiding had not been
wasted.

Suddenly she heard male voices, and recognised them as Lord
Whitestone's and Sir Edward's. What bad luck she was having!
she thought. Well, there was nothing for it but to sit quietly and
hope they would pass by without noticing her.

"Blast it, it's all very well your calling on the Marlows today and
making chitchat with Miss Jane, but what have you learned?" the
marquis was demanding.

"As I was telling you, she is an amazing young lady," said the
baronet blithely. "Demure as you like, sitting there in her
parlour. Scarcely looks like the sort who'd clap Trimble over the
head with her fan and call her sister to task for slighting their
cousin."

"That is the very matter I asked you to inquire about," Lord

Whitestone said irritably. "Has Miss Arnet come to London or hasn't she?"

"I've just seen Miss Land, and she asserts that she has."

"I don't give two farthings for Miss Land's opinion. It's the Marlows who'd know the truth of it!"

"They didn't say," came the answer. "I could hardly come right out and interrogate them, now could I, Jeremy? I suppose I shall have to visit them again, and often. Since we're going to the come-out ball next week, we'll have plenty of opportunity to be around them."

"I'd forgotten about that," Lord Whitestone muttered. "Look, Ned, you're a queer sort of duck. Been turning the subject all evening to keep off Miss Arnet. Is there something you're not telling me?"

"Not at all," said the baronet. "But I will say this. If Miss Jane Marlow is as fond of her cousin as she appears to be, I'll not cross her. Not until I tire of her company, at any rate, which judging from my past should happen any moment now."

The two friends laughed. "Now we'd better look at that new cabbage rose we were sent in here for," said Sir Edward. Gratefully, Marianne noticed from the voices that the men had turned away.

There were murmurs of dutiful appreciation from the pair. "Best we go tell Mr. Jones what a lovely addition she's got to her rose garden, and then be off," said the baronet. "It won't do to keep Prinny waiting."

"Curse it, there's dirt fallen into my shoe," said the marquis. "This wouldn't happen if we wore our trousers and boots for evening dress, but no, we must parade about in breeches and slippers like our grandfathers."

"Nonsense, you're merely out of sorts," said his friend. "You clean your shoe out and do something with your spirits as well, and then come and join the rest of us."

As his footsteps receded, Marianne briefly debated revealing herself but decided not to risk it. Now, if only Lord Whitestone would go away quickly.

She heard a scuffing sound and then a thump, and suddenly a spurt of dust shot her way. Although she turned her head quickly, she was too late; some particles invaded her nose, and she sneezed mercilessly.

"Good heavens!" Lord Whitestone was beside her in a trice. "I don't believe it. You cannot be here."

Marianne decided to make the best of her situation. "I told you, did I not—"

"Yes, yes, that you might turn up anywhere at any time, but I certainly didn't expect to take you literally." His lordship was staring down at her with a look of mingled consternation, mistrust, and pleasure.

Marianne stood up. "I shall go away again if you like."

"How did you get here?"

She nodded at the side door. "It is unlatched."

"Yes, but how did you know I would be here?"

She laughed. "Why, Madame Cransky read it in her cards, of course."

"I own that although I know I am being tricked, I cannot imagine how it is being done," said Lord Whitestone.

Marianne, bathing in the warmth of his nearness, felt her wits momentarily desert her. "How is it that I can outfox you so very cleverly, my lord, and then when you are near me I haven't a thing to say but mere prattle? I find I only want to stand and look at you."

"You are very frank," he said.

"One can afford to be when one is in disguise," she said. Then, as he started to speak, she held up one gloved finger to silence him. "Do not ask my name, but I shall give you one, although I do not promise it is my own."

"Yes?"

"Marianne."

"Is there no more to the name? No surname wandering behind, or are you merely Marianne, like some heroine of the opera?" His words were light, but the tone was serious underneath.

"Will you be at Almack's tomorrow night?"

Puzzled, he nodded.

"Then you shall learn the last part of my name there, although I do not promise it is real, either," Marianne said.

"Impossible." His lordship studied her speculatively. "One

66

cannot enter Almack's without a voucher from one of the patronesses."

"I have obtained mine already," said Marianne. Indeed, with Celia's and Will's connexions, securing the letter had not been as difficult as she had feared. No one had thought to question whether Will did in fact have a sister, for why would he lie in such a matter?

"You tax my credulity," said the marquis. "If you can deceive even Lady Jersey and her lot, I shan't feel so shamed at being hoodwinked myself."

Neither of them had much taste for words after that. Marianne could not resist reaching up and touching the high cheekbones and gazing into the dark brown eyes. Almost at the same time, the marquis's hands went to her trim waistline, and they stood there silently, just touching, breathing the fragrance of each other's presence.

He brought his head down and rubbed his cheek along hers. Marianne closed her eyes and felt him pull her against his hard body. She had no wish to move, ever, only to stand close to him here in anonymous bliss.

He drew away at last, regretfully. "I fear I have promised our prince to join him at Carlton House by half past eleven," he said, the words coming roughly, as if he were unused to speaking. "Even I cannot keep our sovereign waiting with impunity."

"I shall see you tomorrow night," Marianne said. "Truly." Then, not wanting the agony of watching him walk away, she hurried out the side door.

The marquis clenched his fists as he watched her go, yearning to catch her back and hold her, to force her with kisses to tell him the truth about herself. This game was maddening, and ordinarily he would not have tolerated it, but he had felt an urgency in her tone of voice at their last meeting that warned that she did not play lightly, nor without good reason.

He would solve this mystery, this and others.

=7=

AMONG THE CARDS and invitations in the mail the next day was a letter addressed to Miss Marianne Sloan, in an unfamiliar handwriting, on cheap paper. Curious, Marianne took it to a corner of the sitting room.

"My dear Marianne," the letter began in a delicate, feminine hand. "I address this letter to you in the deepest secrecy, for my life depends upon your discretion." This was a strange business indeed! But it was the next sentence that struck Marianne hardest.

"I know that you must be Marianne Arnet, and not Miss Sloan, for Will Sloan has no sister of your age, and he was raised with you." Quickly Marianne turned the letter over to look at the signature, but there was none, so she turned back and continued to read.

"I have information that will clear your parents of all wrongdoing, but my presence here in London must not be known to anyone except you, not even your cousins. Please come by night to see me, and I will give you this proof."

There followed an address that was unfamiliar to Marianne.

Here was a turn of events she had not anticipated. Her parents innocent? Could it possibly be true, or was it a ruse of some kind? She might even be kidnapped, for, after all, she would be going by night, with no word to anyone. If she went.

It appeared that the letter had been written by a woman, and an educated one, but a man could have hired some impoverished governess to transcribe it.

Yet if this person wished her ill, or wished to force money from her, the means was already at hand, for her true identity was known. Since no one in London but her family knew that she and

Will had been raised together, there was only one other possibility that occurred to her. Her parents had indeed given this correspondent some information about her. But for what purpose?

Marianne tried to hide the turmoil in her thoughts as she joined her cousins for tea, but Will was too observant.

"Something is troubling you," he said. "May we know what it is?"

Marianne looked up at him plaintively, unwilling to lie to him but unsure whether she could tell even him about the letter. At last she said, "Nothing I may discuss at this time, Will, although I loathe keeping secrets from you. But it is not my secret; it belongs to another."

Celia nodded. "Well, then, tell me, did you enjoy the company last night? It is too bad you missed Lord Whitestone's visit, for he surely would have been surprised to see you there."

"Oh, but I did not miss it," said Marianne, and related a somewhat edited version of the evening's transaction, glad to be able to confide at least this much in them.

"By the by," Will said when she had done, "I took your new poem to the *Gazette* today and they have suggested that you publish a book of your work."

Marianne stared at him in amazement. "I? A book? Wouldn't that be presumptuous, Will? A girl of eighteen, and no great poet at that."

"Think on it a bit," Celia urged. "The cost would not be great, and surely your grandfather would be happy to bear it."

"Perhaps you might even publish under your own name," said Will. "Think how London would react, to know the talented Mata is in fact Miss Arnet."

Marianne was thinking not of London but of Lord Whitestone. "Not under my own name," she said. "At least, not for the present."

They let the matter stand there, for it was time to take a rest before the evening's excursion to Almack's. Marianne had been looking forward to the outing for some time. She would see Jane there, and perhaps dance with the marquis, and amaze him further with her deception.

Her thoughts, however, would not dwell on ball gowns and gay music. They turned repeatedly to the strange letter she had received. What an unexpected turn of events this was, to hear word of her parents now. Could they truly be innocent? She knew them so little that it had never occurred to her to doubt the evil that had been spoken of them. Even grandfather had admitted that he had seen his daughter so rarely in recent years that he scarcely knew her at all. But if they were innocent, why had they stolen the documents and fled to France?

Restless, Marianne rose at last and let Rachel help her into a low-cut, high-waisted dress of ribbon-striped satin in a soft shade of green that brought out the colour of her eyes. A design worked in the hem and waistband in seed pearls was repeated in the sleeves, and Marianne had fallen in love with the dress the first time she had tried it on.

Feeling slightly better, she descended to join Will and Celia. She determined not to think about the letter hidden away in her room. There would be time enough to think of that later.

The fashionable assembly rooms in King Street were already filled with the haut monde when they arrived. The Countess Lieven and Lady Jersey were among those dancing to Neil Gow's band, and the gaming tables were surrounded with gamblers eager to wager as much as ten thousand pounds in gold coin.

A quick glance about the room told Marianne that Lord Whitestone had not yet arrived, but she saw Sir Edward Beamish waltzing with Jane. Lucinda was dancing with an older man. Priscilla Land stood at one side, fanning herself while a circle of admirers vied in attempting to amuse her.

Will and Celia introduced Marianne to the patronesses as soon as the dance ended, and she was quickly whisked off by a middle-aged gentleman for a Scottish reel. Within a short time, Marianne's dance card was almost filled, but she saved a waltz near the end in hopes that the marquis would arrive.

As she danced a quadrille, Marianne could not help glancing at all these friendly, elegant figures and wondering what their response would be if they knew she was the infamous Miss Arnet. Whoever had written the letter about her parents held the power to embarrass her and her family severely, yet there had been no threat to do so.

Jane espied her and as soon as they could the two cousins went off together in a corner.

"Sir Edward has been to visit every day since Vauxhall," said Jane. "He is the oddest man. One minute he says that he despises all of polite society, and the next he is making up to me."

"I think he admires you, Jane," Marianne said. "But I also overheard Lord Whitestone asking him to keep alert for any word of whether Miss Arnet has in fact come to London."

"I have been spying on him as well," Jane giggled. "Is that not amusing? We shall bump heads in the library some night, creeping about in the dark looking for lost papers or some such."

Marianne forced a smile, then went on. "But have you learned anything in your spying?"

Jane nodded. "Once when he thought I could not hear, he told Mr. Falmby that Lord Whitestone has determined to find out who in London may be secretly supplying information to the Arnets, for he is convinced there are traitors in the Foreign Office itself."

"Do you mean the Arnets continue their infamy even now?" Marianne asked, horrified. What if she were unwittingly to betray her country, through seeking to clear her parents?

"That is what the marquis thinks," Jane said. "It seems the servant who exposed them disappeared soon afterward, and it is thought he may have been murdered by their accomplices."

"Oh, no!"

"However, Sir Edward believes the fellow was merely a loose screw who went to Scotland to escape from gambling debts," Jane said. "Do not refine too much upon it, Marianne. The reports from France are exceedingly favourable, you know. It appears Boney must surrender this spring; everyone says so."

"Let us hope," said Marianne. "Now tell me, what of the baronet? Do you like him, Jane?"

Her cousin nodded, suddenly shy again. "I think I do, Marianne, and I wish I did not, for he is such a good friend to Lord Whitestone, whom I cannot abide for your sake."

"Do not let that interfere with your happiness," Marianne said.

The resumption of the music, and the arrival of their partners for the next dance, cut off any further conversation.

The hour was near eleven, after which no one—not even the Prince Regent himself—would be admitted. Perhaps Lord Whitestone had decided not to come. Perhaps he was weary of their verbal sparring. He might have reconciled with Miss Brinoli and be lounging in her arms even at this moment. Or mayhap he had been accosted by robbers or by French spies and been left bleeding to death in a street somewhere.

So involved was she in her thoughts that it came as a surprise to Marianne when she saw the marquis himself dancing nearby with Priscilla. For the first time that evening, that lady appeared animated, but her partner looked exceedingly bored.

Then his eyes met Marianne's and she saw them widen in surprise. She nodded just enough to acknowledge him. It would not do to speak too openly where others would notice, not yet.

No sooner had she been escorted off the dance floor than Lord Whitestone approached. "I did not truly believe I would find you here," he said. "You amaze me, Marianne. Or are you still Marianne tonight?"

"Yes," she said. "And I promised to tell you the second name I am using, did I not? It is Sloan."

"Sloan," he repeated. "Kin to William Sloan, the artist?"

"That's correct," she said.

The expression on his face changed in some subtle way that she could not quite read. "Kin in what way?" he asked.

She hesitated. Could he suspect the truth? She sensed a thread of anger beneath his civil tone, and yet there was no point in trying to keep her position from him, for he could easily find it out by asking almost anyone. "I am his sister," she said. "Or so everyone believes."

"Does Will believe it?"

"Why don't you ask him?"

She saw him glance up at her cousin's figure across the room. "Clearly he is a participant in this game of yours, and his wife as well, for they have accompanied you," Lord Whitestone said.

The coldness of his tone frightened her. Suddenly he was neither the man who had held her lovingly in his arms nor J., the

72

sensitive correspondent who had roused her dreams for so many months. He was Lord Whitestone, her vengeful, implacable enemy, and he would destroy her if he could.

"My lord, I regret having deceived you," Marianne said, wishing her voice did not sound so small and young. "I—I thought to fix your interest by appearing strange and mysterious, but I am neither of those things. I am simply Marianne Sloan, Will's sister, so you need ponder the matter no further."

He fixed her with a stare so intense that she had to fight back the urge to run away. "I don't believe you," he said. "You were more convincing as a sprite or a gypsy than you are as a correct young lady in society. If ever you were deceiving me, I think it is now."

She could not bear to be kept in ignorance. "Then who or what do you think I am, my lord?"

The marquis shook his head. "I wish I knew. This is a tangled business, Marianne. Will you not tell me the truth now and put and end to it?"

"But I have . . ." She couldn't finish the sentence, couldn't lie again and swear that she was Miss Sloan. "Oh, Jeremy, I cannot!" She realised she had used his Christian name, but there was no going back now. "Please forget you ever met me! I promise not to appear at the Cyprians' Ball—yes, I was even going to do that, and I would have found a way, I assure you!"

"That I believe." His mouth quirked up in a half-smile.

"Nor shall I sell flowers at Covent Garden, nor any of the other things I had planned," Marianne said. "It would be best if we did not talk again, if we became merely polite acquaintances. Whatever you may learn of me someday, please believe it is myself I have done a disservice. Can we not let the matter rest there?"

"Can we?" He was looking at her sharply, and she could not meet his eyes.

"Such intense conversation! One does not see it often at Almack's." Priscilla Land sailed up, twirling her little painted fan. "Why, Miss Sloan, I did not know you were acquainted with his lordship. An acquaintance of some duration, it would appear."

Priscilla's gossiping tongue could do more harm than almost anything Marianne could imagine, and she saw at once that the marquis was annoyed as well. "Yes, indeed," she said smoothly. "We are very old friends indeed. Often we have gone riding on his estates in Sussex."

"Essex," corrected his lordship.

"We rode so very enthusiastically we went all the way to Sussex," Marianne finished.

"Quite true," said the marquis. "Our families have been very close since childhood."

"Whose childhood, yours or hers?" snipped Priscilla.

"They were very friendly indeed during his childhood and moderately well acquainted during mine," said Marianne.

"It was a longtime dream of our mothers' that someday we should wed," said the marquis outlandishly.

"However, they quarrelled bitterly and our engagement was terminated," Marianne concluded.

"You're having a go at me, aren't you?" said Priscilla. "I know perfectly well that not a word you've said is true, either of you."

"Not much of the gossip one hears is true, either," Marianne said.

"How dare—" Priscilla stopped suddenly. "Here comes that vexing Lucinda Marlow, with that missish parson tagging after her. Do you know, Lord Whitestone, she's put it about that you're on the point of offering for her?"

Lucinda had arrived in time to hear this last remark, and reddened furiously. The marquis, however, rescued her by saying gallantly, "I was in fact on the point of offering for her—to escort her in a set, if I may."

"Why, yes, indeed." Lucinda turned and caught sight of Marianne, who had been standing with her back to her cousin. "What are—" She choked off the words. "Miss Sloan. How very pleasant to see you again. I had not realised you and Lord Whitestone were acquainted."

"Oh, they are very old and dear friends," said Priscilla sarcastically. "Their mothers had planned for them to marry, until they quarrelled—the mothers, that is. Did you know that?"

Lucinda's shock was so plain that Marianne and Lord Whitestone both had difficulty restraining their mirth, and after one quick glance avoided each other's eyes.

The marquis sobered quickly. "I did not realise Miss Sloan was known to you," he told Lucinda.

"Why, Lord Whitestone, of course they are!" chirped Priscilla. "Do you not know that the Sloans and the Marlows—"

"Are the very best of friends!" Lucinda and Marianne said in one breath. Drat that Priscilla. If the marquis did not know they were cousins, there was no reason to inform him now.

"And here is Mr. Falmby, come to escort Miss Land," added Marianne, steering that hapless young man to his unchosen partner.

She made good her escape, but only for the duration of the dance. Then the marquis sought her out again and asked for the next one. It was the waltz she had saved and, securing the required permission, she consented with some trepidation.

"You seem to know everyone," said the marquis as he guided her through the crush. "How can your identity be a secret then?"

"It cannot be much longer," she said ruefully. Then his hand was at her waist, and she felt herself melt into his arms. As they circled to the music, it was difficult to restrain the impulse to stand on tiptoe and press her cheek against his.

"I shall discover the truth, I warn you," he said. Marianne blinked at him, dazed for a moment and then brought back to grim reality. "It will be easy enough to make inquiries into the Sloan family, for I believe they are of noble birth, are they not? If Will has a sister, then I shall find out if you are she. If he does not, perhaps I will find some clue as to who you are."

"If I begged you not to do this, for my sake, would you give over?" she asked earnestly.

"You have hinted all along at some dark secret, something quite threatening," said Lord Whitestone. "What manner of man would I be if I did not wish to protect you from it? Yet I cannot, since you will not tell me what it is."

They were back in their endless circle, Marianne thought. He could not protect her because he himself was the danger, and she could not ask his help because to do so would place herself and her family in jeopardy. Now especially, with the arrival of the letter that implied her parents might be both innocent and in peril, she could not risk discovery.

"Suppose I were to go away?" she asked. "If I were not under-foot, so to speak, you would have no reason to enquire after me."

He guided her through the waltz for a few moments before replying. "Would you truly do that? Go away and never see me again, to hide this secret of yours?"

His grip on her hand and waist tightened, and the masculine power of his nearness robbed her for a moment of speech. Then she whispered at last, "If it were only I . . . not willingly, my lord. But it may come to that."

Tears stung at her eyes and she turned her head aside. His voice was husky when he said, "Marianne, I did not mean to distress you. But I cannot bear this . . . this minuet of pretences. It goes against my nature. If you vanish, I shall follow you and find you out, so there is no advantage in that."

"If I stay, will you promise not to delve into my past?" she asked, still not daring to look up.

"Will you in turn promise to tell me everything, as soon as you may? Or shall that never happen?" he asked.

"Yes, I hope it will," she said. "I shall tell you the truth as soon as I can, but I do not think you will like it."

"Do you think me so inconstant?" he asked.

Once again, for a moment, she was tempted to tell him every-thing, until an image flashed into her mind of the relentless hatred he had shown at Vauxhall when the Arnets were men-tioned. "Perhaps I wish you were less constant," she murmured, adding quickly, "It would be best, as I said, if we were to become mere acquaintances."

"Is that what you wish?"

"With all of my mind, and none of my heart," she said as the waltz ended, and dashed off to ask the Sloans to take her home.

=8=

ALONE IN HER room, still in the ribbon-striped green satin gown, Marianne reread the letter. "I have information that will clear your parents of all wrongdoing, but my presence here in London must not be known to anyone except you, not even your cousins. Please come by night to see me, and I will give you this proof."

What proof could there be? she wondered. The word of the servant who had informed on her parents? But she would not know him if she saw him.

Yet as she looked at the blank space where the signature should be, it occurred to Marianne that perhaps what the letter did not say was as revealing as what it did. There were no threats to expose her, nor demands for money. There were no extravagant promises —such as the presence of that servant—which might have tempted her. There was no false name, such as might easily have been signed. All pointed to the sincerity and earnestness of the anonymous writer.

Anonymous letters do seem to be playing rather an important part in my life these days, Marianne thought with a wry smile. She copied down the direction and returned the letter to her drawer. At least if she did not return, they might know where she had gone, and why.

She changed quickly into a dark-blue bombazine gown with a matching pelisse, and tucked some coins into her reticule. A quick glance about the hallway told her no one was near. Will and Celia had remained downstairs, and most of the servants were abed.

Marianne slipped down the back staircase unnoticed and out the rear door, leaving it unlocked so that she might reenter without raising the household. It took her some minutes of walking before she spotted a hackney and gave it the direction, but soon she was on her way. She jounced uncomfortably on the carriage's creaking springs, and hoped the worn squabs were not home to hordes of fleas.

The building was in a poor area near the Haymarket, and fear crept through Marianne as she considered the lateness of the hour and her own unprotected situation. When the hackney clattered to a halt, she considered for a moment telling the driver to take her home again. But she knew she would never dare to return if she left now, so she told the man to wait for her and let him hand her down, trying to ignore his curious expression.

She stepped into a narrow hallway, wincing at the unpleasant odours. From one side, she heard the sounds of a man and woman quarrelling and a baby crying.

Resolutely, Marianne made her way up the stairs to the third floor, groping uneasily in the darkness. What would Lord Whitestone say if he could see this? A welcome glint of humour told her that at least he would have to admit that the mysterious Marianne was true to her word: She might turn up almost anywhere.

Swallowing hard, she knocked lightly on a battered door that she hoped was the right one. At first there was no sound from within, and she thought her mission had been in vain. Then she heard a rustling noise and light footsteps, and the door opened.

She blinked in the sudden light, although it came from a single candle. Then Marianne stared at the thin, tense woman's face above it, and gasped.

"Mother!" she said.

"Marianne!" Quickly Mary Marlow Arnet opened the door and pulled her daughter inside, encircling her shoulders and pulling her close. "Oh, Marianne, you did come! I didn't dare to sign my name. It was so dangerous to write you at all! And I hated to bring you here, to this terrible place, at such an hour, but I had to see you!"

"Mother, what are you doing here? Is Father here?"

"No, he remains in Paris."

Lady Mary lit another candle and urged Marianne into a chair.

Her daughter glanced around, dismayed by the dismal surroundings, the bare walls and tattered curtains, the rickety bed and cracked mirror.

"Mother, why are you staying in such a place? If you have left Father, if you were innocent, you must tell Grandfather."

"I have not left your father," Lady Mary said nervously. "I shall be bringing Jean-Pierre here as soon as it is safe."

"I don't understand." Now that the first rush of emotion was fading, Marianne found herself torn by conflicting sentiments. She wanted desperately to believe what the letter had said, that her parents had done nothing wrong. But perhaps her mother meant that they had done nothing wrong by their beliefs, which supported Napoleon. Still, it made no sense for her mother to have come to England. Even if they feared an allied invasion of Paris, she would have been safer in some foreign country.

"No one must know of this," Lady Mary said grimly. "No one must know that I am here, or why, or what your father is doing in Paris. Not even the Foreign Office."

"I should think you would say *especially* not the Foreign Office," said Marianne, bewildered.

"Yes, I keep forgetting how little you know." Her mother passed a hand over her forehead wearily. "I wanted to tell you but it was too dangerous. One cannot expect a child to keep such secrets. I'm sorry, Marianne; you have suffered for our work and until now you have not even known why."

"Mother, please explain what is going on," Marianne said. "In your letter, you said you had proof of your innocence."

Lady Mary coughed into her handkerchief, then smiled ruefully. "My proof is that I am here. Let me start from the beginning, and then you will understand."

"I should like that very much," Marianne said.

When Mary Marlow first met Jean-Pierre Arnet, she was impressed by his easy and charming manners. As she came to know him, she discovered that beneath this polished surface lay a deep, abiding conviction that his homeland was being destroyed. Gradually she came to share his concerns for the battered and bruised France.

It was after their daughter was born that Napoleon seized power. Arnet, who had already been keeping an ear cocked during his business trips abroad, intensified his attempts to learn more about this dictator who soon crowned himself emperor.

After war broke out, some of Arnet's connexions in the Foreign Office asked to formalise the relationship, albeit secretly, by having him convey to them whatever he could learn of Napoleon's plans and weaknesses. Lady Mary, anxious to be close to her husband and knowing her presence would help shield his purpose, accompanied him to the Continent—although they never dared enter France itself—even though it meant leaving Marianne with relatives.

"Do you mean you were spying for England?" asked Marianne, amazed and relieved.

"Yes, but it was kept a very grave secret, as you can imagine," said her mother. "We dared not even tell my father. In the Foreign Office itself there were those with loose tongues, and gradually word might have reached some traitor and ended in our deaths. Only a few men knew about us."

Arnet managed to build himself up in the confidence of some French diplomats by persuading them that he was in fact a sympathiser with Napoleon. At last the time came when they asked him to spy for them in England.

"Surely he told them that he could never betray his wife's family in such a way!" Marianne protested.

Lady Mary shook her head. "This was a very valuable opportunity, Marianne. We discussed the matter with our contacts and devised a plan."

It was determined that what was needed was a spy inside France, as close to Napoleon as possible. Both of the Arnets agreed to undertake this perilous task, and so a scheme was developed.

An agent of the British government was employed as a temporary servant in the Arnet household. It was arranged that secret papers be stolen from several houses where the Arnets were visiting and planted in their residence. The next time they went abroad, the "servant" betrayed them, and they were denounced as traitors to England.

This move convinced the French that the Arnets had indeed undertaken their spying mission and were loyal to Napoleon. As a result they were accepted into the circles of his government.

"You mean you have been spying for England?" Marianne gasped. "Oh, Mother, if only I had known!"

"I wish we could have told you," said Lady Mary sadly. "But we feared to put too great a burden on you, such a young girl and such a very deadly secret. That was my only regret in the matter, that you must think the worst of us and suffer for what others thought."

"But then why are you here now?" asked Marianne. "Why has Father not come with you?"

"He is now embarked on the most dangerous project of all," said her mother.

Although enemy forces were closing in on Napoleon in this March of 1814, it was by no means clear that their victory would be accomplished without a terrible bloodbath, perhaps even the destruction of Paris itself. Arnet saw the greatest task of the war before him: to persuade the officials of the city to sign a treaty with the allied forces as soon as Napoleon had left Paris to command his armies.

In this way, the city itself and many lives might be saved. But in order to plead his case, Arnet must reveal that he was not entirely sympathetic to Napoleon, and thus raise some questions as to his presence in France.

"He insisted that I go away," said Lady Mary. "I have grown thin with worry, and the excuse was made that my health suffered and I must go south. Jean-Pierre urged me to stay in Italy, but I could not abide to be there alone, afraid for his life and with no way to tell you what was occurring. So I came here."

"But surely the Foreign Office could find you better lodgings than this!" cried her daughter. "How very grim this all looks, and you not well!"

Lady Mary sighed. "We are not dealing directly with the Foreign Office, through any official channels," she said. "Our connexions there are themselves under surveillance, for it is believed that they secretly aided us. They dare not reveal the truth at this critical period, for there are real spies as well, whose identity is not known to us."

81

"This is Lord Whitestone's doing!" Marianne said. "It is he who brings pressure to expose your supposed fellow traitors, he who single-mindedly hates my father!"

Quickly she told her mother all about the marquis, his letters as J., his missive to her grandfather, their meetings in society, and his hatred of the Arnets.

"It is best then that I remain here, and that you not come to visit me again," said Lady Mary. "It is enough that I know you are well, and that you at least have been told the truth about us."

"You must think me a poor daughter indeed, to imagine that I would leave you here, alone and near penniless!" said Marianne. "I shall visit you as often as I may, and I will try to obtain better lodgings as well."

Lady Mary's eyes were wet with tears. "I am deeply touched by your offer. I had feared to find you distrusting, resentful. But Marianne, it is possible we will be seen if I am moved. I do not fear so much for myself as for you. If you are seen aiding me, you will be branded a traitor, yet we must reveal nothing while your father remains in France."

Marianne hesitated. She had borne being labelled the daughter of traitors, because there had been no choice, but how could she bear being thought to be one herself when it was not true? Jane would be humiliated, and Grandfather. Lord Whitestone would look at her with such loathing . . .

She pulled herself up straight. It was his fault too, she thought, that she paused even a moment in doing what she knew to be right because she had seen how even the suggestion of scandal could hurt those she loved. But in this there could be no compromise.

"I assure you I will do all that I can to help," she said. "Are you sure I may not tell Will and Celia? You know they would do anything, too, that they could. You would be safe at their home."

Her mother gave a small, dry laugh. "And are there no servants in this home? No one who might carry the tale? How innocent you are, Marianne. These last few years, I have learned more than I had ever dreamed of treachery and suspicion. In France, I could confide in no one, no one at all. There were no friends, only those who might at any moment become enemies. This is how you must learn to see things now."

"Surely Will and Celia—"

"Perhaps they themselves are harmless, but the more who know a secret, the less a secret it becomes." Lady Mary broke off and coughed so violently that she doubled over. Marianne could only wait helplessly until the fit was ended.

"Mother, you cannot remain here," she said firmly. "I shall find some way to secure you a better home, even if I must sell my pearls and anything else I own of value."

"Marianne, you must not arouse suspicion." But her mother, coughing again, could not argue for long.

"I promise you, I'll think of something," Marianne vowed, although she hadn't an inkling what scheme she might devise. "And I shall bring you warmer clothing and better candles. Tomorrow night."

Lady Mary took a sip from a cup of water on the night table. "My sweet daughter, how much I have missed watching you grow up," she said. "But promise me you will not come if it is perilous. I will understand. I fear for your safety even now, coming and going at this hour of the night."

"I have asked the hackney to wait for me," Marianne said. "Don't worry, Mother."

Reluctantly, she said good night, and returned downstairs, feeling bathed in sunshine in spite of the shadowy darkness of the building. Her parents were innocent! They were heroes, not traitors, and they loved her very much. That had been the hardest part, believing that they had not cared what happened to her or how she thought of them. Now Marianne felt that she could brave anything.

Her mood evaporated quickly, however, as she emerged into the street to find it empty. The driver, no doubt despairing of her return, had not waited.

Marianne considered for a moment returning upstairs to stay until morning, but she realised that such a tactic would surely arouse alarm in the Sloan household and require explanations that she would be unable to give satisfactorily. She must find her way home.

Clutching her reticule tightly, she began walking toward what appeared to be a larger street to her right. Her footsteps echoed with unnatural loudness through the emptiness of the night. At this hour of the evening, hardly anyone dared venture abroad save robbers and cutthroats.

Marianne turned a corner but found she was in a street just as narrow and winding as the one she had left. She continued on and turned again, and soon was so well and truly lost she could not have found her mother again for all the spice in India.

The sound of wheels and the clop of hoofs made her turn. At the sight of a stylish phaeton, her spirits rose. Here was a well-bred young man who would surely aid her.

But as the carriage drew closer, she saw the man eyeing her bawdily. "Well, well, what have we here?" he called, pulling his team of horses to a stop. "A young lady, or shall I say a wench? Out for a stroll, are we? Like some company?"

He dropped heavily to the ground and grabbed for Marianne's arm. She turned and ran blindly, hearing the horses stir as the man jumped back into the phaeton and started after her.

Now where could she flee? This could not truly be happening, and yet it was. She was racing down a street in the worst area of London late at night, with a debauched man chasing her, bent on her ruin.

Marianne dashed around a corner and found herself in a larger street at last, with voices wafting out from public houses and intoxicated men and women sauntering about the street together. Her pursuer was forced to rein in his horses to avoid running down some of the strollers, and Marianne was able to gain some distance on him.

She glanced back and heaved a sigh of relief to see that he was driving off in the other direction. Then a hand clamped down on her arm and she turned in alarm.

"Thought ye'd got off, did ye?" A large, beefy man, his nose red from drinking, held her in an iron grasp. "Don't ye know this here's the territory o' Joshua Raines, and any young woman what comes 'ere unaccompanied is me property?" He leered at her and laughed as she tried to twist away.

"Eh, don't fight it, ducky," said a henna-haired woman lounging nearby. " 'e's a good boss, 'e is. Don't 'ardly beat 'is girls 'cept when they 'old out on 'im."

Marianne bit her lip. This man was worse than a debaucher. She didn't know the word for such things, but she knew he was a man who turned helpless young women in prostitutes, and there didn't appear to be anyone here on this street who would stop him.

"You take your hands off me!" she snapped. "I'm the grand-daughter of Lord Marlow and he'll have the Bow Street Runners on you!"

"Oh, it's the granddaughter of an earl, is it?" mimicked the fat man. "And I'm the Emperor of China, I am!"

There was raucous laughter all around, but it died away sud-denly and Marianne heard light footsteps approaching. Her captor tightened his grip so she couldn't turn to see who it was.

"So!" challenged an elderly female voice. "I've warned you, Mr. Raines. I don't interfere in your doings unless I'm asked, but you're not to be forcing any innocents into your filthy way of life." Her very welcome champion reassured Marianne, and the voice sounded very familiar.

"I've no mind to take orders from ye, Grandma Pointynose," growled the man. "This 'ere chicken come running into me arms, she did, an' she's fair game for me."

" 'ey, look out, Josh, Grandma'll put the evil eye on ye, she will," warned the red-haired woman in frightened tones.

"Ye remember Sam 'arris?" asked a man nearby. "She done it to 'im, and next day a carriage run over 'im in the street an' broke both 'is legs."

"I ain't afraid of nobody," said Joshua Raines. "But this 'un ain't no good to me anyhow. She's a scrawny mite." He pushed Marianne away from him roughly, and she would have fallen except for a pair of reed thin arms that caught her.

"Oh, thank you," Marianne said, and looked round to find herself staring into the eyes of Fritzella Crane.

"Marianne!"

"Miss—" Realizing Fritzella might not want her name spread about, she halted, then went on more cautiously, "So this is where you go of an evening."

"Let's be off," Miss Crane said, and Marianne realised quickly that the corpulent Joshua Raines might even now change his mind.

They hurried away, arm in arm, Marianne not daring to look back. "Oh, Miss Crane, I was never so glad to see anyone in my life!" she said. "That horrible man—I told him I was the granddaughter of an earl, but he just laughed at me."

"A good thing too," said Miss Crane. "If he'd believed you, I've no doubt he'd have held you for ransom. You don't know the ways of these sorts, Miss."

In the next street, Miss Crane halted in front of a rough wagon. Reaching up, she shook the shoulder of the dozing driver, who woke with a start and stared around him wildly for a moment before realising where he was.

"Hssht, Rob!" Miss Crane said. "Wake up now, lazybones! Time to take us home!"

The man nodded dazedly and as soon as they had settled themselves on the straw-filled bed, the wagon creaked its way back to Clarence Square.

"What an odd conveyance," Marianne said. "But serviceable. I ordered my hackney to wait, but he did not."

"Probably feared for his life," said her companion calmly. "Rob here's the son of an old friend. For a few shillings, he takes me wherever I ask, and waits, too. In one of his previous lifetimes, he was a charioteer in Rome. In this life, he's a baker's assistant. Such are the mysterious workings of Providence."

Marianne, who had been engulfed by a feeling of unreality ever since escaping with Miss Crane, began to shiver as the memory of her recent danger seeped back. Fritzella pulled a scratchy blanket around the two of them.

"Speaking of the mysterious workings of Providence, what were you doing in such a place at this hour?" Miss Crane asked. "Not that I'm nosy, no indeed, but a person can't help wondering."

"I was . . . visiting a sick friend," Marianne said carefully. "Someone who, well, doesn't want her whereabouts known just now. You have to believe me, Miss Crane, there's nothing smoky about it, but you see, I've sworn to help her and keep her secret, so I can't tell anyone, not even you, or Will or Celia."

Miss Crane nodded. "I thought you was a kindhearted miss, and I see I was right. Now, Marianne, I shan't pry, but you must vow to tell me if there's any way I can help."

Marianne nodded, wishing she could unburden herself to this wonderful, eccentric old soul. Instead, she asked, "What were you doing here? That man seemed to know you. He called you Grandma Pointynose. Oh, dear, I hope I haven't offended you by repeating that."

"Not at all." The wagon hit a pothole and jounced the pair of them into the air, but Fritzella's demeanour remained unperturbed. "I come here often."

"Into that street of . . . of cutthroats and worse?" Marianne gasped. "Then you must be brave indeed."

"Not brave," Fritzella said. "But I have a long memory."

"I beg your pardon?"

"It was in Babylon," Miss Crane said. "Yes, I believe Babylon. Or perhaps in Egypt? I am getting old, aren't I?"

"Never mind where it was," Marianne said reassuringly. "What was it? I don't even know what we're talking about."

"Babylon," said Fritzella decidedly. "That was when I was forced into a life of sin. Terrible thing, terrible. Let me tell you, Miss, it ain't changed much in all these centuries. For every Serena Brinoli sauntering about in satins and jewels, there's a hundred of 'em walking the streets or shivering in some cold room, poor brutalised little creatures."

"You were one of those once?" Marianne asked. "How painful that must be to remember."

"That it is," said Miss Crane. "So I determined to do something about it in this life, since it's the only one I have at the moment."

They stopped just then in a lane that ran in back of the Sloan house. The two women piled out, and Miss Crane handed Rob some coins before waving him on his way through the night.

"I've left a side door open," Marianne whispered.

"Shouldn't have done," said Miss Crane. "Be murdered in our sleep, we might. I've got a key."

"But I haven't, and no excuse to ask for one."

"Then we shall have to go out together, shan't we?"

Marianne felt greatly comforted.

She followed her companion up the narrow steps to the attic, where Fritzella brewed a pot of herbal tea over her small stove.

"Pray finish your story," Marianne said as she warmed her hands on the steaming cup, inhaling the fragrance of cinnamon and cloves. "I remember you and that man were talking about your interfering with his business. Is that what you mean?"

Miss Crane nodded. "I'm in the business of rescuing fallen women," she said. "Only those that want to be saved, mind. This is no religious thing, although perhaps there's a bit of that in it as well. It's for my own peace of mind, you see."

"What do you do with these women?"

"There's a small house I've got not far from where we met, that I inherited from my sister," Fritzella said. "There's women there who've been with me for years. They teach and care for the newcomers, who learn skills, and sew and knit for their keep. We find them stations in life, or keep them with us as need be."

An idea warmed Marianne far more than the tea could have done. "Miss Crane!" she said. "Do you have room for another one? For my sick friend, I mean. She's not exactly a fallen woman, but she is in great need, and very worthy."

Miss Crane nodded. "Say no more, Miss. I'll let you know the first night Rob's free to take us. Maybe even tomorrow."

=9=

THE NEXT DAY, as had been previously arranged, Marianne went to visit the Marlows at their home in Grosvenor Square. Jane had been most anxious to consult her on the preparations for her come-out ball the following week, and even Lady Marlow had to admit that Marianne's presence in London so far had not resulted in any harm.

She, however, had not seen the gypsy girl at Vauxhall Gardens. But Lucinda had, and there was a reckoning to be made.

"Whatever mischief are you about?" she demanded as soon as the girls were alone in the library, with the guest list and menu for Jane's ball spread before them. "You almost gave the game away before Lord Whitestone's very nose, and ruined us all!"

Marianne hesitated, beginning to realise that she hadn't thought this matter through as well as she had believed. How could she reveal to Lucinda that she thought it in her power to captivate the marquis, when Lucinda was persuaded he was in fact enamoured of herself? She dared not tell of the stolen kisses, either, for the same reason.

Jane came to her aid. "She means to throw him off the scent!" she said. "Can you not see, Lucinda, that spying her about with us at times and with the Sloans, whom Priscilla knows to be our cousins, might give us away? But seeing her here and there, dressed as a gypsy, perhaps, one day and a lady the next, he thinks the whole of it is a masquerade, and her an odd prankster. Even should someone reveal her as Miss Arnet, it is possible he will not believe it, but will think it is just another of her tricks. Do you not think that is as good a scheme as any?"

"Grandfather would be furious," retorted Lucinda. "And what would Mother say?"

"They both agreed to my pretending to be Miss Sloan, did they not?" said Marianne mildly.

"Oh!" Jane clapped her hands to her face. "Do you know what I have remembered? Sir Edward is to call upon us at teatime, and no doubt Lord Whitestone will be with him. Mother is taking the carriage to Lady Jersey's and Father has the curricle, so you must stay here with us, Marianne, for we have no way to send you home. What shall we do? I swear I will not hide you away in a broom-closet, not in my own home!"

"There, you see?" sniffed Lucinda. "Had she not paraded herself about and called herself to his attention, he would pay no mind to a Miss Sloan, but now he will certainly ask questions. And that horrid Priscilla Land has been quizzing everyone as well, and no doubt will quickly help him uncover the truth."

"You do not expect Priscilla, I hope?" Marianne asked.

Her cousins shook their heads. "But she does come to visit at the most awkward times!" said Jane. "If she suspects that Lord Whitestone is to be here, she will devise some pretext for coming as well."

Marianne sighed. "I could take a hackney home," she said.

"You will not," said Jane. "What a nasty thing. I am sure those hackneys are filled with insects of every variety. Moreover, you are to stay to supper, and Father will be furious if he finds out we packed you off because of Lord Whitestone. He is much like Grandfather in his sentiments, you know."

"He never thinks of me at all," said Lucinda. "Of us, I mean. For all he cares, we might spend the rest of our lives in a convent."

"Why should he think of us?" challenged Jane. "It is our honour at stake here. I would do anything to help Marianne, and as for Lord Whitestone, if I were Father, I would forbid him in the house."

"No doubt you would give a come-out party for Marianne as well, under her own name."

"Yes, I would! And you would feel the same way if you had any pride at all!"

"Cousins, please!" Marianne interjected. "I pray you not to

quarrel because of me. We had best put our heads to solving the problem at hand."

"We could say we are all ill, and send a message they are not to come," suggested Jane.

"Ill?" Lucinda glared at her. "Then we should scarcely be recovered in time to attend the Lands' breakfast tomorrow, and Priscilla will have a clear field with all the men."

"Wait." Marianne held up her hand. "I have an idea. I had resolved not to continue my—my masquerade, as Jane so aptly phrased it. But perhaps one last time would do no harm. I shall pose as a parlourmaid, and assist in the serving. That will amaze everyone."

"And outrage Father, should he hear of it," said Jane.

"But it is a lark," Marianne said. "I am not disgraced or degraded if I am only playing a game, am I? I have heard of titled ladies doing such things in jest, and it was well taken all round."

"There will be questions, surely," said Lucinda. "No one will truly believe you are a servant."

"I do not wish them to," said Marianne. "Say merely that I am a most eccentric acquaintance, and when I learned one of your maids had taken ill, I asked to take her post for a day, so that I might learn what her life is like. Say that I write novels, and wish to make a character study."

Jane laughed. "I think it great fun, do not you, Lucinda? Surely Lord Whitestone would never suppose us to parade Miss Arnet before him in the guise of a serving girl!"

"In that I suppose you are correct," Lucinda said. "Very well. Now let us get on with our planning. Do attend and stop giggling in that odious manner, Jane. Shall we have lobster patties at the ball supper?"

The afternoon passed quickly. The complicity of the housekeeper was quickly assured, although she was understandably dubious at first, and the housemaids thought the idea a great joke.

The only discomfort for Marianne was being unable to confide in Jane about her mother. She felt disloyal keeping such a secret, but she had given her promise. Moreover, she was beginning to understand what her mother had meant. Had she been free to tell those she trusted, she would already have revealed the truth to

Will and Celia and Miss Crane and Jane, and possibly Lucinda as well. That was five people, five tongues that however well intentioned might let slip some hint in the presence of the wrong person. Unquestionably, the wrong person was the marquis himself, she thought grimly.

Marianne's pale hair was gathered into a demure bun, and she donned the starched black dress and white apron lent her by one of the maids. A few instructions were given by the housekeeper, and Marianne practiced a quick bobbing curtsy.

She stood in the kitchen listening to the guests arrive for tea. There were more than expected, for Mr. Falmby came. She heard him hesitantly address Lucinda, and sensed his disappointment as she dismissed him with a brief greeting and turned her attention to the next set of arrivals.

They were, by the voices she now knew so well, Lord Whitestone and Sir Edward Beamish. Ned's tones became animated as he addressed Jane, but the marquis sounded bored with the whole business.

Last came Priscilla Land, pretending surprise at seeing the other guests and at learning that she had come at the precise hour for tea. Lucinda was obliged to invite her, although her tone was barely civil.

At last the bell was rung. The housekeeper led the way with a silver tray containing the teapot and cups. The head parlourmaid followed with the sandwiches and cream and Marianne brought up the rear with a plate of cakes.

It was strange to view the drawing room from the perspective of a servant. Marianne, who had spent much of her childhood feeling very much the outsider, had never considered how she might look to a maid. Probably very spoiled and arrogant, she thought humbly.

Lucinda, Jane, and Priscilla struck her now as far more glamourous than they had ever seemed before, and their voices tinkled brightly, like fine crystal bells. The gentlemen were all much handsomer than she remembered, and Lord Whitestone, with his dark good looks, quite took her breath away.

They were discussing the situation in Paris, and whether it would collapse or the troops be forced to destroy it street by street before attaining victory. Priscilla's comments were frivolous in the extreme. She regretted that the best dressmakers' shops might be ruined. Do we always sound so vain and foolish? Marianne wondered.

"Even if they surrender, is there not the possibility of treachery?" inquired Mr. Falmby. "I mean to say, they might be forced to sign a treaty, and then attack our men in the streets."

"One must always be on one's guard," agreed Sir Edward. "Having served on the Peninsula with Jeremy, I have had a taste of treachery. But I do not think the Parisians at heart hate the English. It is this Napoleon who has led them wrong. He is some sort of devil, I am convinced of it."

"He has a devilish effect on England as well," said Lord Whitestone.

"Whatever can you mean?" asked Priscilla, clearly only too happy to goad him to speak ill of the Arnets and distress their hostesses.

"There is no need to discuss particulars," said the marquis stiffly.

We might as well be invisible, Marianne thought as she and the other servants set the food down. The others had not even glanced at her face. She had never thought she and her acquaintances were so indifferent to those who served them, as if they were sticks of furniture.

"Oh, please, Lord Whitestone, you cannot leave the subject without explaining yourself," said Priscilla, her voice oozing concern. "What effect can Boney be having in England, save to rouse us all to patriotism and unite us against him?"

"We are not united!" Lord Whitestone said. "There are traitors in our midst, even within the Foreign Office itself."

Marianne, who was in the process of handing him a cup of tea, deliberately dropped it into his lap. At this, Lord Whitestone uttered a curse and jumped to his feet, mopping himself with his handkerchief. The others in the room expressed varying degrees of dismay, with the exception of Jane, who was having a hard time stifling her glee.

"Oh, sir, I do beg your pardon!" said Marianne. "Do let me help, please." She seized a serviette from the table, ignoring the fact that Mr. Falmby had only just placed a cake upon it, and began rubbing at the marquis's clothing. The result was to leave a smear of cream and crumbs across the front of his fawn-coloured jacket.

"Blast it, woman, have you no—" Lord Whitestone stopped in mid-sentence and stared at her openmouthed. "Good heavens, it's you. Whatever are you doing dressed as a maid?"

"I am trying to clean up this mess you have made of yourself," said Marianne in as scolding a tone as she could manage. "If you have no manners, sir, you should not frequent drawing rooms, you know."

"Capital!" cried Sir Edward. "She's having a go at you, Jeremy, and a sorry sight you are, too!"

For a moment, his lordship hovered between outrage and mirth. Fortunately, the latter won, and he chuckled along with his companions. "I am a miserable wretch, am I not? Assaulted in the Marlows' drawing room! Priscilla, I have no doubt you shall spread this story all over London, much to my discredit."

That lady appeared most displeased with his frame of mind. "Indeed, my lord, I should hardly think you would take it so lightly," she said. "The damage to your coat is considerable."

"The damage to my self-importance is even greater," he said amiably. "Tell me, Miss Sloan, how do you come to be parading as a maid? I had thought you said you were relinquishing such performances."

"So I had intended," Marianne acknowledged. "But I learned—do not ask me how, for I shall not tell you—I learned that you were coming here today and proposed to play a trick on you. Miss Marlow and Miss Jane are not without a sense of humour, and agreed to play along."

"Much to the detriment of my apparel," said the marquis. "Now you must do a better job of cleaning me up, Miss Sloan."

"I beg your pardon?" She gazed up into twinkling brown eyes. "Oh, well, let us go in the kitchen, then."

"You most certainly will not!" said Lucinda. "Lord Whitestone is not to descend into the kitchen. Take him into the library, Marianne, and I will have water and cloths brought to you."

"Do try not to spill any more on him, will you?" giggled Jane.

94

No sooner had the housekeeper departed, leaving Marianne and the marquis alone in the library with a bowl of water and a pile of cloths, than she realised she had been cleverly manoeuvred.

"You could have sent your coat to be wiped without your person in it," she observed as she set to scrubbing a spot, intensely aware that she was pressing against a thin layer of cloth over a firm, well-muscled chest.

"I could have done," agreed his lordship. "But then we should not have had this, should we?"

Before Marianne realised what he was about, Lord Whitestone had caught her shoulders and tipped her chin up towards him and was kissing her quite thoroughly. She tried to pull away but he held her tightly, and after a moment she acquiesced and leaned against him happily.

All she could feel at that moment was the warm desire in his mouth and hands, the hardness of his body against her and the overpowering masculine scent of him. Enclosed in his embrace, she was transported to a new world of longing.

"Marianne." His voice was husky as he lifted his head and gazed down at her. "You are a maddening woman."

"Am I?" She pressed her cheek against his coat. "My lord, I assure you, it is I who am outwitted and outrun."

"What?" he teased. "Here I stand with tea and cakes spread upon my coat as though it were a picnic cloth, and you wish me to believe that I have got the best of you?"

"But you have," she murmured. "I had not meant to tease when I dropped the tea on you. I meant to make you angry."

He drew away slightly and regarded her with curiosity. Marianne, coming out of her fog, realised she was on the verge of giving away her secret, and perhaps her parents' lives. After all, she had no reason to wish to antagonise Lord Whitestone, not so far as he knew.

"Why did you wish to do that?" he asked.

"I . . ." She gazed at him and a logical explanation came to her. "You were flirting so outrageously with that horrid Priscilla Land, and I simply could not abide it."

"Jealous?" he asked with a touch of wonder. "I had not expected that."

"Why not?"

"You are so independent," he said, as if examining each word before releasing it. "So . . . ethereal, at times. Somehow I had not thought human emotions could capture you so easily."

She turned away, not wanting him to see her confusion. "I am only human, after all," she said.

"Are you?" Hearing the edge in his voice, she looked back at him. "Then why do you insist on remaining so mysterious? Marianne, I think it is time you explained to me what this is all about."

At that moment, Marianne would have given her pearls and gowns combined to have had some interruption, but none was forthcoming. What could Lucinda and Jane be thinking of to leave her alone with him this way? But no doubt they believed the housekeeper had remained in the room, and Marianne had not thought to insist that she stay.

"My lord—"

"Please call me Jeremy. You have done that before, you know."

"Jeremy." She hesitated. "I cannot tell you."

"Why not?"

"Because it is not my secret. It belongs to another."

"I have never heard of any secret that requires a young woman of good breeding, with an acquaintance such as yours among the nobility, to go scampering about London dressed as a gypsy or a parlourmaid, and to spill tea and cakes upon a lord of the realm."

Marianne hesitated. She could not even promise to tell him at a later date, for she could not set one. It must be after the fall of Paris, and he must not suspect that she had any connexion with France.

"Or perhaps . . ." His voice darkened with quick anger. "Perhaps this is merely a wager you have made."

"It is not a wager," Marianne said. "What would the purpose of that be?"

"To bring me to the point of offering for you," said the marquis. "It has been tried before. Are you an actress, then? Perhaps some of our friends, even the Marlows, who have no reason to think well of me, believe it great sport to make a fool of me."

"I assure you that is not—" Marianne stopped. It was indeed her point to make a mockery of him, but not quite as he supposed.

"Is not what?"

"There is no wager, my lord," she said. "I am not an actress, and I do come of good family."

"But your name is not Marianne Sloan."

"No, it is not."

"You are not Will Sloan's sister, either?"

"No."

"I am at a loss," he said. "I tire of this playing. Perhaps your motive is revenge. Is there some wrong you fancy I have done your family? Some brother of yours who died in the war under my command?"

Marianne walked across the room and stopped with her face toward a window. He had touched too close to the truth for safety. He had only to think one step further to realise who it was in all of England who had the greatest reason to wish revenge on him.

If only she dared declare that she was indeed an actress, and this had all been a wager! But he would continue to see her with the Sloans, and must realise she had lied. Or she could invent some wounded brother or cousin, but he would only place the blame on Arnet rather than himself, and she was not sure she could contain her temper.

Had it not been for her mother's presence in London, she might have given up the task she had set for herself and returned to the country. But she could not even do that now.

Marianne glanced over at where the marquis stood waiting, with a puzzled look upon his handsome face. In that moment it washed over her: I am in love with him. The one man I can never have. What a nodcock I have made of myself.

"I cannot explain the reason to you even now," she said in as level a voice as she could manage. "Nor can I leave London, as I might wish to do, to spare us both embarrassment of meeting again. But you need not think, my lord, that you have been made to look foolish. If you could see inside my heart—" Tears threatened her composure. Marianne dashed out of the room and up the stairs without waiting for his response.

As they rode away later in Sir Edward's curricle, Lord Whitestone maintained a silence that piqued his friend.

"Come now, Jeremy," Ned protested. "You have not said a word of what transpired between you and Miss Sloan. All a body knows is that you came back looking as if you'd been to your mother's funeral, and Miss Sloan vanished entirely. Have you murdered her and hidden the body between volumes of Chaucer?"

The marquis did not even smile. "What occurred must remain between the lady and myself," he said, then added softly, "May the Lord help me. The wench is driving me to distraction."

"I would hardly phrase it so strongly," said his friend. "It is you who drive ladies to distraction. Did you notice how Miss Land and Miss Marlow all but fought for your attention? Yet you scarcely spoke a word to either of them the rest of the time."

"There was hardly room for me to speak, with you chattering away," said Jeremy, recovering a shadow of his spirits.

"What, me?" Ned chortled. "It is that Jane Marlow who is the problem. The minx was so merry the whole time I could scarcely keep from laughing myself. I do think the sight of you dressed in tea and cakes did wonders for us both."

"I fear this coat is ruined," said the marquis as his friend guided the horses round a corner. "But it is of no moment. I told you I should not have come today."

"You are too much buried in business these days," said Ned. "You have been in the House of Lords for five years but never have I seen you take such an interest in affairs of government as you do now."

"Never saw reason to," Lord Whitestone answered.

"This Arnet business," said Ned blithely, undaunted by a glare that would have felled a less sanguine chap. "You've grown positively rabid on the subject these last weeks. *L'affaire Arnet* transpired fully two years ago. Why take so great an interest now?"

"I am not concerned with what is dead and gone, but with what is in the wind this very hour," said his companion. "I was surprised to find that many championed the cause of Miss Arnet, reproaching me for my stand in the matter."

"But she is merely a chit of a girl. And she has grown up in England, Lord Marlow's granddaughter. Surely your suspicions are exaggerated."

"Her mother grew up in England, too, and she was Lord Marlow's own daughter," replied Jeremy. "No, Ned, you are an innocent when it comes to politics. There are many sympathisers with Napoleon, and some who do more than sympathise. They are growing desperate, and they must be found before they commit acts of outrage in London itself."

"In London?" Ned gaped at him as the curricle halted in front of Lord Whitestone's house. "You cannot mean . . ."

"An assassination? It is entirely possible." The marquis stepped down onto the street. "Do not speak of this to anyone, Ned. It would not do for the wrong people to realise how suspicious we are."

"Of course not." The baronet shook his head wonderingly. "Here in England? Bloody bad business, Jeremy."

The marquis sighed wearily as he watched his friend drive off. Walking up the steps and being ushered inside by the butler, he allowed himself to indulge for a moment in dreaming.

If only he might go to his club tonight and spend a peaceable evening gambling with his cronies. Or perhaps visit his box at the theatre, and watch for Miss Sloan, or at least enjoy a performance by Edmund Kean. He might even, could he give his full attention to it, unmask the mysterious Marianne and learn this deep secret that loomed so large to her and which, he was sure, would seem impossibly insignificant to him, if he could only win her trust enough to lead her to confide in him. Women refined so heavily on matters of small moment.

But tonight he would do none of those things, Jeremy reflected as he allowed his valet to undress him and gave orders that supper be served him on a tray. Tonight he must play spy. Not play, he reproved himself as he cleaned and oiled his pistol and secured it inside his waistcoat.

The net was tightening around the traitors in the Foreign Office. Soon they must give themselves away, and some, he suspected, were quite high ranking. Papers had disappeared, an English spy in Dover had been found stabbed to death in his room at an inn, and a cache of rifles had been commandeered from a ship in the channel and no doubt taken to Boney.

Then there was the matter of the ship from France that had arrived only a few nights before. Someone had been aboard that ship, someone of considerable importance who had been spirited away quickly to a point in London. This much his watchers had learned, but no more.

There was no doubt in the marquis's mind that this person was a trained assassin, the person brought to wreak as much damage in England as possible. The Prince Regent had been warned, and was heavily guarded, as was the prime minister, but there were countless other targets. Even me, Jeremy thought.

Two nights before, one of the men most under suspicion at the Foreign Office had been traced into a section of the Haymarket where such a person had no business going late at night. There could be no doubt he had taken information or supplies, or both, to the assassin. Unfortunately, his trackers had lost the trail, and the man had not gone out the next night.

It was likely he would return tonight or tomorrow, however, and this time Lord Whitestone did not intend to let anyone lose sight of him. There would be no failure, and he would make sure of it, because he himself was going to track the traitor.

=10=

A SMILE BEGAN to twitch at the corners of Serena Brinoli's mouth and spread until it threatened to split her face. She read the note one more time and then looked up at the seedy fat man who stood before her in her yellow salon.

"You've done well, Joshua," she said.

"I'll 'ave me payment then, Martha," he answered, grinning as the sound of her true name made the elegant woman before him wince.

"Here," she snapped, tossing a small pouch of coins at him. Insultingly, Joshua poured them into his hand and counted them before turning and whistling his way out of the room.

Serena breathed a sigh of relief after he was gone. Although she might have summoned her butler to cast him out, she'd no wish of bad blood between her and Joshua Raines. The man was scum but he was powerful scum.

Then she remembered the note and her good humour was restored. So Will Sloan had never had a sister, and Lord Whitestone was being played for a fool. He wouldn't be so enamoured of that little flirt after he heard this news.

The information about Mr. Sloan, coupled with Josh's certainty that "Miss Sloan"—the name of the false gypsy girl Jeremy had deserted Serena for—was the same young woman he had caught running down the street the previous night, could mean only one thing. The chit was an imposter, an actress or prostitute pretending to be a lady. Somehow she had hoaxed or blackmailed the Sloans into providing her with a false identity so that she might snare his lordship as a husband. Well, she hadn't reckoned with Serena Brinoli.

Martha Bowkes—for that was her real name, although she had long since discarded it—knew full well she was unlikely ever to reclaim the marquis for herself, but at least she might have the satisfaction of seeing her rival similarly discarded.

Tonight, Serena intended to confront Grandma Pointynose and learn the truth. The old woman lived in the Sloan household and had rescued the chit from Joshua, and she surely knew all that was to be known. Serena had learned the location of her house in the Haymarket, and through her groom had determined that the young bumpkin who drove the old crone had been summoned for that evening.

She debated whether her next step should be to confront the false Miss Sloan and force her to write the truth in a letter to Lord Whitestone, or whether it would be best to induce Grandma Pointynose to accompany Serena on a visit to the marquis. Best of all would be to witness in the flesh the farewell scene in which his lordship denounced the scheming wench and she raged against him, telling him her true—or revised—opinion of his worth, as Serena would have done under the circumstances. Still, one could not hope to actually witness such a scene, since it might not be possible to arrange for a personal confrontation.

Serena mounted the stairs, calling for her maid. She planned to dress at her ease for what promised to be a most enjoyable evening.

Marianne went up to bed early that night, then changed quickly into sombre clothing. Although Miss Crane might come and go as she pleased at any hour, there would be questions asked if Marianne were to do the same, even in her chaperone's company. Therefore, it had been decided that she should pretend to retire, then join Fritzella in the lane behind the house.

So it was that, perhaps three-quarters of an hour later, Marianne found herself in the cart with Miss Crane, clopping back toward the Haymarket.

Although she felt some concern at venturing again into that cut-throat region of London, her primary feeling was one of relief. Against all hope, she had found a place where she might entrust her mother and know that she was well and cared for, without revealing the truth.

They arrived at Lady Mary's address without difficulty, and Marianne excused herself, explaining that she must go up alone.

"She is frightened of strangers, and might be thrown into a panic were she to see you without explanation," Marianne said. "Let me put it to her alone, and then we shall come down and join you."

She hurried upstairs, her heart thumping wildly. What if her mother had fallen severely ill in the night? What if she had been discovered, or her connexions had felt it best to remove her to some other lodging?

Marianne tapped at the door and waited. At last she heard her mother's voice ask warily, "Who is it?"

"It's I, Marianne," she said.

The door opened swiftly. "Oh, thank heaven," said her mother. "I was becoming frightened."

"Why?" Marianne slipped inside and embraced her mother. "Has something happened since last night?"

Lady Mary shook her head. "Not yet. But you see, when my friend from the Foreign Office came the night before, he told me he had been followed. He managed to lose his pursuer, but he was unsure when he might be able to return. He said perhaps tonight, but he has not come, and I thought mayhap he could not come again at all, or else that I should find myself hauled off to prison."

"All the more reason we must flee quickly," said Marianne, "although I do not see why this friend of yours could not have found you a more tolerable place to await him."

"This was the only room that could be found quickly and without questions being asked," said Lady Mary, who looked even thinner and more haggard than she had the night before. "Once here, I dared not venture out, so money was of no use to me, and he could bring only small packages of food and clothing without attracting notice."

"Well, I have good news," Marianne said, chafing her mother's cold hands between her own. "I have found a safe place to take you, where you will be cared for, and no one will question you."

Lady Mary gave her a look of mingled hope and doubt. "I cannot imagine that such a place exists. Marianne, I have told you, even the best homes have servants who might—"

"It is not like that, mother." A note of excitement crept into Marianne's voice. "An elderly woman of my acquaintance, Miss Crane—she was Will Sloan's wife's nurse—has established a home for women who . . . who wish to reform, women who have been . . . women of ill repute."

Her mother looked at her with an unreadable expression.

"Miss Crane believes it is her mission to rescue these women, clothe and feed them, and help them to earn their living honestly," Marianne hurried on. "She has a home near here, very clean and safe, so she says. I told her I had a friend in need, and she agreed to let you stay there."

"Marianne, I do not mind poverty," her mother said hesitantly, "but to sink so low, to stay among such women—" a fit of coughing wracked her body and she was unable to finish.

"But you must have proper care!" Marianne urged. "Mother, you will die here; you cannot stay here alone! I will not let you! If you go to prison, you would die there as well. There is no other choice for you. It cannot be so bad, and I shall come as often as I may."

At last her mother nodded. "You are right, my child," she said. "This is no time for false pride."

Her pitifully few belongings were quickly gathered up and a cryptic note left for her Foreign Office friend should he arrive, and the two descended to the street together.

Lady Mary quailed for a moment at the sight of the rude cart and the beak-nosed old woman who perched jauntily on the straw in back, but then she consented to be assisted up beside her.

"M . . . Mary," said Marianne, "this is Miss Crane, who is known hereabouts as Grandma Pointynose. Miss Crane, this is a very dear friend of mine, whom I hold as dear as my own mother. Her name is Mary."

To her credit, Fritzella asked no questions, not even her new acquaintance's surname. "You do not look well," was all she said before ordering Rob to drive on.

They had gone but a short way before Marianne spotted the

figure of a man hastening down a side street, his furtive movements indicating he did not wish to be observed. Her mother caught her gaze, followed it and uttered a gasp. "That is . . . that is my friend who was to visit me tonight," she whispered. "He looks as if he is being pursued."

"Then surely he is headed home, for safety's sake," said Marianne. "I am glad we were not forced to delay to another night, for I cannot bear to think of you alone there without sufficient food and warmth."

Again, Miss Crane watched and listened but said nothing. Perhaps she had noticed a resemblance between the ailing woman and Marianne, the girl thought, or perhaps she had simply learned discretion from years of helping those who had many things to hide.

Suddenly a man on horseback dashed around a corner and nearly bowled into them. The horse reared, whinneying, and Rob was hard put to hold even his ancient nags from bolting.

"What the deuce are you doing with a wagon out at this hour, man?" shouted the rider. Then, in a moment of shock, Marianne looked up and met the furious eyes of Lord Whitestone.

He stared at her for some moments before he found his voice. "Good lord, Marianne, what are you doing here?" Then he frowned. "I do seem to be asking that a lot, don't I?"

Marianne was uncertain how to respond, but she wanted to warn her mother of the man's identity as quickly as possible, so she said, "It comes as something of a surprise to me also to encounter you here, Lord Whitestone." She heard her mother's quick indrawn breath beside her.

"If I'm not mistaken, that's Madame Cransky, who I've learned is also known as Miss Crane," observed his lordship. "I'm glad to see you're properly chaperoned, but dash it all, Marianne, it isn't safe for a young woman to be out in this area at such an hour, chaperoned or not."

"We are on an errand of mercy, sir," said Miss Crane. "I assure you, I would not expose Miss Sloan to any more peril than absolutely necessary."

Lord Whitestone hesitated, glancing up and down the street. "I say, have you seen a man slinking about? Medium height, wearing a blue greatcoat? You'd know him in this area, for his clothes are well made.''

"We've seen no one of that description," said Marianne.

"Blast! I've lost him."

"What business is this, my lord?" she asked, taking the offensive. "Are you engaged in some havey-cavey stuff? Or is this one of your gentlemen's wagers, perhaps?"

He opened his mouth, seemed to think the better of what he was about to say, and finally answered, "Yes, something of the sort. I appear to have lost my bet."

"Then perhaps you had best go about your business, and we shall go about ours," said Miss Crane. "Drive on, Rob."

To Marianne's dismay, the marquis rode along beside them as they clattered over the rough street. "Surely you don't suppose I would leave you here unprotected, now that I've found you?" he said, studying her with a puzzled expression. "Do Will and Celia Sloan know where you are?"

Marianne shook her head. "No, and please don't tell them, for they'd only worry needlessly."

"Yes, but suppose you should come to some misfortune," said his lordship earnestly. To Marianne's relief, he was paying no attention to Lady Mary, who kept her eyes lowered demurely. "I should be much to blame for having said nothing."

"My lord, there really is no need to watch over me," she said. "Truly, Miss Crane would expose me to no harm."

He lifted an eyebrow. "Or perhaps this has something to do with that little secret of yours. Parading about as a gypsy, a parlourmaid, and heaven knows what else, and here you are mysteriously clattering about the Haymarket late at night in an old cart. Are you a smuggler, Marianne?"

"Oh, indeed yes," she teased back with feigned lightness. "We are smuggling straw, as you can see, sir."

The wagon halted before a row house that looked much like all the others about them, and Marianne felt a knot of apprehension. The appearance was not unduly dilapidated, but neither was it particularly well kept, and she hoped she had not put her mother to so much discomfort and risk only to transfer her to some equally dismal spot.

Lord Whitestone insisted on handing them down, and the irony was not lost on Marianne as he assisted Lady Mary to the ground. What a news report this would make, were it known that her archenemy had lent aid to the infamous French spy. If Marianne and her mother were exposed, he would never forgive them for this, Marianne thought, allowing herself one wistful peek at his handsome face.

To her humiliation, the marquis intercepted the look and stepped toward her protectively. "If your errand is completed—" he began.

"Not quite," interrupted Miss Crane. "If you will await us here, your lordship; there are no men allowed in this house. We will return shortly."

As soon as they had entered, Marianne's fear eased. The hallway was spotlessly clean and the wood well oiled. Even Lady Mary's face brightened slightly as she took in the impeccable furnishings, mended carpets, and crisp draperies.

"Elizabeth! Sarah!" Miss Crane called up the stairs. "We have a new resident and she is ailing. Come down, please!"

Marianne heard rustlings above them and then two women came down the stairs in their nightclothes.

"Oh, she do look tuckered!" cried one, taking Lady Mary's arm. "She no be one o' us, though, do she, Grandma? She's not got the look of one 'at's lived the street life."

"Mary has been equally unfortunate in her own way," said Miss Crane authoritatively. "She's to be put to bed at once, and fed, and not required to do work until she feels considerably better. If she coughs badly, you're to fetch the doctor, Elizabeth."

The young woman nodded. "But there's no need to worry, Grandma. We've not forgotten all the good ye done us. We're more'n 'appy to 'elp a fellow sufferin' creature."

"You're very kind," said Lady Mary.

"Now don't keep Mary standing about," said Miss Crane. "Off you go!"

"No, wait, please!" said Lady Mary. "May I have a word with Marianne in private first?"

"Of course," said Miss Crane. "Sarah, tell me about Lydia. How has she been since she came?"

"Well, mum, it's only been two days . . ."

They moved off, and Lady Mary spoke in a low voice. "Do you think he is suspicious?" she asked anxiously. "I had not thought to encounter Lord Whitestone himself."

"It appears my nonsense of running about in disguises has put him off the scent," said Marianne. "He thinks this is another of my jests."

"But surely the man must suspect something," her mother persisted. "He must learn if he does not already know that the Sloans are your cousins. Soon he will put the pieces together."

"We can only pray that Paris will surrender first, and Father be safe, and then all can be told," said Marianne. "It is a wager against time. Now, Mother, I hope you will try to rest here and be comfortable. I know what sort of women these women have been—"

Her mother smiled gently. "You were right earlier to remind me to be humble," she said. "I warrant each of them has a story that would break your heart. No, I am feeling properly grateful for such pleasant shelter."

Miss Crane returned, and Lady Mary insisted on walking back with them to the door. "I may not see Marianne again for some days, and I am loath to part with her," she said.

As soon as they opened the front door, Marianne knew that something had gone astray.

The street had become quite crowded, for beside the wagon and Lord Whitestone's horse stood a fashionable chaise, and in it sat none other than Serena Brinoli, wearing a triumphant expression.

"So!" she cried. "I had not expected to see you so boldly together, Grandma Pointynose and Marianne! You see, my lord—"

"I see nothing but that you have filled your head with jealous nonsense," said the marquis irritably. "Marianne, this wench has been telling me Will Sloan has no sister."

"I told you that myself," said Marianne.

"She is a great pretender!" cried Serena. "I've no doubt she is an actress, and a clever one at that. Mincing about and pretending to be a lady! Why, she's a common harlot!"

All might yet have been saved had not her words so infuriated

Lady Mary that the woman spoke up angrily. "How dare you!" she retorted. "You have no right to speak of my daughter in this manner!"

For a moment everyone stood frozen. The cat is out of the bag now indeed, thought Marianne miserably. There was nothing for it but to tell the truth—what Serena Brinoli thought was the truth, anyway.

"I fear Miss Brinoli is correct, my lord," Marianne said, catching her mother's hand and squeezing it as a caution to remain silent. Indeed, there was no need. The whiteness of Lady Mary's face testified that she was aware how foolishly she had endangered their whole precarious scheme.

"Is this woman your mother?" asked Lord Whitestone, head cocked to one side in curiosity.

"Yes, she is," said Marianne. "I am bringing her here because she is destitute and has nowhere else to go."

"Truthfully, Marianne?" he asked quietly.

"Lord Whitestone," she said, swallowing hard. "I fear my great secret has been revealed. I am not a lady. I was . . . I was myself a girl of the streets until two years ago, when Miss Crane rescued me and set me on the right path."

"There!" crowed Serena. "What did I tell you?"

"Put a damper on it!" snapped the marquis. "Continue, Marianne."

"She brought me here." Marianne prayed that the house had been in existence two years ago, or that if it had not, no one would give her the lie. "At that time I had been separated from my mother and did not know her whereabouts."

"A pitiful little thing she was too," interjected Miss Crane, joining the tale. "You're not to blame Marianne for the sort of life she led, my lord. If you'd seen how ill she'd been used—she had great bruises on her body, and walked with a limp."

Marianne felt herself flushing scarlet and was grateful for the darkness. "There's no need to provide his lordship with intimate details of my physical state," she said. "But, my lord, I gradually learned to conduct myself like a lady, and improve my speech." She remembered at this juncture that she must somehow account for her mother's excellent speech as well. How on earth did people manage to lie all their lives? It was infernally complicated! "I had no difficulty doing so, because my mother had been a gentlewoman before her unfortunate marriage."

The marquis watched her with open skepticism. "You haven't explained how the Sloans came to take you in and introduce you about as their sister, and present you to their acquaintances, and obtain a voucher for you at Almack's."

I cannot invent so quickly! Marianne wanted to retort, and bit her lip. However, her mind was working more rapidly than she would have supposed possible, and so she continued.

"It was my goal at first to become a governess, and later to run my own school for orphan girls," she said. "But Miss Crane believed I would benefit by greater exposure to polite society, and so she prevailed on the Sloans, for she is Mrs. Sloan's former nurse."

"There you have it!" exclaimed Serena. "By her own confession, she is a fraud! Now what do you think, my lord?"

"I think the whole tale is preposterous," said Lord Whitestone. "I do not believe a word of it. Marianne is not a wanton and has never been one. Whether this lady is her mother I cannot decide. I must suppose that she presumes herself to be, for she spoke with some conviction in defending Marianne against you, Serena."

"But if this is not all true, what do you suppose this chit to be doing in this area, at such an hour?" protested Miss Brinoli. "How do you explain her pretenses? I'll tell you what she did not confess, Jeremy. She determined to ensnare you. Perhaps the Sloans took her in innocently, meaning to help with a worthwhile enterprise, but this woman is a fortune hunter. She meant to hoodwink you, have no doubt!"

"If that is the case, she has chosen an odd way to go about it," said the marquis. "A trollop masquerading as a lady would certainly not dress up as a gypsy and a parlourmaid to attract my interest. Miss Crane, I would not expect a woman of your station to be party to such deviousness, but then, I must remind myself you were got up as a gypsy as well."

Lady Mary sagged against Marianne, and the girl hurried her up the steps and into the house. As she handed her mother into the care of Elizabeth and Sarah, Marianne tried feverishly to think of some explanation that the marquis would believe, but she could think of none save the truth. And that must not be told, no matter if she herself were to go to prison.

She emerged to find the marquis wearing a triumphant smile. "I have it!" he declared. "I shall accompany you home, Marianne, and there I shall confront Will Sloan. He may have introduced you into society for reasons of his own, but he is an honest man, and I believe he will tell me what lurks behind all this."

With a sinking feeling, Marianne took her place in the cart. It was true that Will was unlikely to lie; at best he would refuse to own the truth. But how would he feel when he learned she had been traipsing about the Haymarket late at night? He would have a perfect right to be angry, and in his wrath he might let slip the truth.

As they rattled forward, Marianne felt very much like a French aristocrat during the Reign of Terror, rattling through the streets of Paris in a tumbril, headed for the guillotine.

═11═

IT WAS A motley entourage that halted in front of the Sloans' establishment in Clarence Square: Serena Brinoli chortling in her chaise, Lord Whitestone barely subduing a grin as he sat on his dashing stallion, and Marianne huddled miserably beside Miss Crane in the back of the cart.

She entertained brief hopes that the butler would announce that the Sloans had retired for the evening and were not to be disturbed under any circumstances, but such was not the case. Will and Celia customarily remained awake late, reading and talking, and so they were doing tonight.

They came to the door, their surprise evident at seeing such an assemblage, especially Marianne.

"I thought you had retired," said Celia in some bewilderment. "What are you doing going about at this hour, Marianne?"

"And you, Miss Crane," said Will. "You were to accompany Marianne on her escapades, not lead her into them."

"Let us not stand about in the street," said Celia. "Come in, Marianne, Miss Crane, Lord Whitestone." She gave Serena Brinoli a skeptical look. "And you are?"

"She is on her way home," said the marquis firmly. "Are you not, Serena?"

The dark-haired woman glared for a moment at being cheated of her reward, but even she was not insensible of the fact that polite families did not invite members of the demimonde into their drawing rooms.

"Indeed, I have expended far too much time in attempting to save you from your own folly," she said, and signalled her groom to take her off. Rob and his cart jounced after her.

"I apologise for disrupting your evening," said Lord White-stone as they entered the hall.

"It appears there is much here of which we should be informed," said Will, fixing Marianne with a puzzled stare.

She looked unhappily down at the floor. She had never intended to hoax Will. Indeed, she was fully aware of how great a favour he had done by permitting her to come and stay with him in London, and how great a risk he had run. She prayed that he would not reveal everything to Lord Whitestone, for that would imperil not only the Sloans' social standing but that of Jane and Lucinda, which would be most unfair. And her mother, of course, might pay with her life.

"Perhaps we should speak alone," said Marianne. "There are some things I wish to convey to my cou—to Will and Celia in private."

The marquis's face hardened in sudden anger. "I have not come here to be treated in such a ramshackle fashion!" he said. "I have been tricked and lied to and made a fool of in front of my friends, and now I will have the truth of it! Will, I am given to understand that you have no sister."

"That is true," he said apologetically. "Lord Whitestone, I agree, it is time we laid our cards upon the table. I believe you should hear the full tale from our mouths, and not by chance from some gossips."

They sat stiffly about the drawing room, waiting for the butler to pour a glass of claret for the marquis and then be gone. Marianne kept her eyes focused on her hands, except for a sidelong look at Celia to beg for understanding.

"Now," said Will when the butler had gone. "Before we begin, Lord Whitestone, would you do me the favour of telling me how you came to encounter this pair tonight, and where they were and what they were doing?"

"I was about some business of my own," said his lordship. "Imagine my astonishment upon espying these two riding about in a rough cart in the Haymarket."

"The Haymarket!" cried Celia. "At this hour!"

"Precisely," said Lord Whitestone. "There was with them a third lady whose name I do not recall."

Everyone looked at Marianne. "Mary," she said, and saw Celia's puzzled frown deepen.

"Yes, some poor gaunt-looking woman, although she spoke in a most genteel manner," said their narrator. "I accompanied them to a house in . . . I did not note the street, I fear, although I believe I could find it again. There this lady was deposited and Serena Brinoli, that . . . that woman whom you met with us, arrived also with fantastic claims about Marianne's being some sort of actress all got up to trap me into marriage."

"I can assure you there is no truth in that," Will said.

The marquis nodded. "I did not think there was. At any rate, this gaunt woman I mentioned became quite angry and told Serena she had no right to insult her daughter in this fashion."

Celia gasped and Will paled.

"I see this comes as something of a shock." Lord Whitestone studied them intently. "Is this woman her mother? Why was she going about London in such shabby garb and at such an hour, being smuggled about in a straw-cart, so to speak?"

Neither of the Sloans seemed to be able to speak. They looked at each other in disbelief and then both turned to gaze at Marianne questioningly. She quickly returned her gaze to her lap.

"Perhaps it would be best if you told the entire story from the beginning," suggested the marquis, who was also looking at Marianne.

"Well . . ." For the life of her, she could think of no way out of this one save fainting dead away onto the carpet, and she did not see how she could manage that.

She opened her mouth and then closed it again, watching the golden flecks glint in his dark brown eyes. She had only to say a single sentence, a sentence that would reveal her name, and this lean, handsome, maddening man would stand up and walk out of her life forever. She would never again hear his deep rumbling laugh, never again feel the touch of his hand on hers or his lips pressed against her cheek, never see him come striding up with a welcoming grin.

At that moment, there was a soft rap on the door, and the butler opened it slightly. "There is a gentleman to see Lord Whitestone," he said.

"Me?" The marquis rose, surprised. "No one is aware of my whereabouts this evening, I believe."

"Forgive me, Jeremy." It was Sir Edward Beamish who hurried into the room. "There is a matter of some urgency, and we are all fanned out to search for you. I thought perhaps, since you seemed to be nowhere else, that you might be here."

"Clever thinking," said Lord Whitestone drily. He turned to his hosts. "Please forgive the intrusion. I beg you to excuse me."

"Of course." Will nodded, and Marianne sank back onto the sofa in relief.

She heard whispers in the hall and caught only a few words. One of them was "spy" and another was "confessed." Marianne's blood seemed to have solidified in her veins, and she thought that surely the marquis would return at any moment to accuse her of treason and order her to accompany him to gaol.

But he merely stepped in to say that urgent business required his departure. "We shall finish this most enlightening conversation at another time," he said. "I trust that is agreeable to all parties, Marianne?"

She looked up at him pleadingly. "If you require it, my lord, then I suppose I am forced to consent. But we will none of us profit by it, least of all you."

"Allow me the privilege of judging for myself," he said, and was gone.

They all waited until the sound of hoofs had faded away, and then Will spoke. "I think you had better tell us what has happened, Marianne. Is your mother truly in London?"

She nodded. "Miss Crane, I should have explained to you. My mother . . . she is not what they think . . ."

"Your name is Arnet, I believe Will said when first we met," said Miss Crane. "I am not such a fool as never to have heard of the Arnets. But I do not believe what is said of them. Remember when I told your fortune with the Tarot? I said someone far away was watching you and caring about you. It was your parents."

"But this is madness!" said Celia. "She will be caught! Lord Whitestone himself has seen her! Why did you not tell us, Marianne?"

"She begged me to tell no one. She feared to endanger us all.

115

But she is so ill, and her lodgings were so shabby, so when I learned that Miss Crane maintains a home for reformed harlots, I—"

"She does what?" Will looked at the old woman with mingled astonishment and admiration. "I had wondered where you went of an evening, Miss Crane, but I had never expected an activity so . . ."

"Charitable?" suggested Miss Crane, and he laughed. "But you remember the house in Boar's Lane where my sister resided when she was alive? I have kept it up to good purpose."

"But Marianne has not explained what Mary is doing here in England," said Celia. "Surely she cannot be spying, not all alone and ill. Has Jean-Pierre deserted her then, cast her out? Had she nowhere else to turn?"

Marianne stood up and walked to the door, opening it and looking up and down the hall to make sure no curious servant was standing with an ear to the keyhole. She was, she reflected, learning to be suspicious of everyone, just as her mother had warned.

Satisfied, she returned to the room and sketched the situation quickly—her father's true role and loyalty to England, his determination to help save Paris by persuading its leaders to surrender behind Napoleon's back, and his concern for her mother's safety.

As she spoke, Marianne found herself pacing up and back on the carpet, her hands gripping the folds of her skirt. "But now what is this business that has called Lord Whitestone away? Did you not hear them mention a spy and a confession? Perhaps someone has told the truth."

"It cannot harm you," observed Miss Crane. "For the truth is that your parents are loyal British subjects."

"But it can harm my father!"

Will frowned. "It seems more likely that they have located a French spy, and that he has confessed what is known to him —which would be that your parents are agents of France."

"Then my mother is in danger!"

"There can be no question about it," said Celia firmly. "Your grandfather must be told. If your mother is indeed in danger, then he must use all his influence to keep her out of prison, where she would surely die, until your father can accomplish his mission and the whole of it be revealed.''

"Mother will be very upset," Marianne said. "Now there are four of us who know, besides her, and with Grandfather there will be five, and soon servants will learn of it. What a terrible business this is! How very difficult her life must have been all these years, having to hide and lie to everyone, even those she loved. How very brave and patriotic my parents have been, and all this time I believed the worst of them!''

"You should not blame yourself," said Will. "You knew no more than the rest of us. I shall send for your grandfather directly, although I do not dare entrust this story to a letter. He must hear it in person.''

"Do you truly think he can help?" asked Marianne, forcing herself to sit down again but perching on the edge of the sofa. "He has such a hot temper. Will, I fear he will be enraged when he sees how ill she is and learns that she is being cared for by women of such .   . such low station. He may reveal everything in his fury!''

"We have no choice, dear," said Celia.

Miss Crane, who had sat silent through most of this exchange, nodded in agreement. "Too much of a burden has been placed on your young shoulders, Marianne," she said. "I saw it in your cards, that you are a woman of honour who never seeks to impose upon others, but this is not a matter any of us can resolve alone. Your grandfather is entitled to know that his daughter has returned, and that she is innocent.''

Reluctantly, Marianne agreed. Only then did she realise how extremely weary she was, and so excused herself from the room.

"This time, I trust, you truly mean to retire and not go gallivanting about the streets?" said Celia with mock seriousness.

Marianne nodded. "I was so very frightened, the first time I went to see Mother, quite alone. It was only by good chance that I encountered Miss Crane. I suppose I should say, it is good chance all around that I made Miss Crane's acquaintance.''

She and the older woman smiled at each other. "But it is not mere chance," said Fritzella. "We have met in former lives, you and I, Marianne.''

"How about Lord Whitestone? Have I met him before?"

"I can tell you this: you shall certainly meet him again," said Miss Crane enigmatically, and Marianne went upstairs.

She did not wake Rachel, preferring to undress by herself. As she laid her gown across a chair, her eye fell on a letter that had been placed on the table beside her bed.

Marianne blinked at the familiar handwriting, which seemed somehow out of place. Then she realized it was J.'s.

How could it have come here during her absence without someone's realising she was gone? She searched her memory and vaguely recalled Rachel saying something earlier in the evening about Mr. Sloan's having been to the *Gazette*. No doubt the abigail had placed it there and, in her worry over her mother, Marianne had failed to observe it.

Hesitantly she sat on the bed and opened the letter. She had not replied to Lord Whitestone's previous missive, and yet she was very glad he had written again. She wondered if, even after the marquis learned her true identity and spurned her, she should tell him she was Mata as well. It would be foolish to cling to a friendship that must mean so much to her and so little to him, and yet she did not think she could bear for it to be broken off entirely.

"My dear Mata," the letter began. "It saddens me that I have not heard from you, although no doubt you are, as you said, removed from your dwelling, and will not receive my last letter or this one until you return.

"You will note, from reading that document, that I have encountered a most fascinating, yet disturbing young lady who continues to baffle me. She maintains that some dire secret prevents her declaring her true identity. Half the time I am persuaded this is mere nonsense, that she is only shy due to my title. Half the time I believe she refines too much on some minor matter. Half the time I am convinced she is a wicked persuader who tries to ensnare me, and the rest of the time—but there is less than none left, is there? Never mind. The rest of the time, I begin to believe she speaks truly, and there is some mystery I cannot guess at."

Marianne paused, pleased to know that he thought about her so much and at the same time feeling a twinge of guilt, as if she were spying on his innermost thoughts or eavesdropping on an intimate conversation. Yet all in all she could not resist reading on.

"Fate seems to conspire against me, for although I have made mild attempts to uncover the truth, some happenstance seems always to intervene." Fortunately for me, thought Marianne. "Were it not for other business of the gravest nature, which must needs occupy much of my time and thought, I should have resolved this matter long ago."

Were it not for that business with France, there would have been no mystery for you to solve, she thought.

"I ask you, as a woman, to tell me this. Could a woman who loves a man deceive him in this manner, or are such arts reserved exclusively for ladies whose affections are not engaged? Whatever my feelings for the lady in question may be, I must know if there is a chance they are returned. You can understand that I would not wish to devote myself to the pursuit of her secret, only to learn that she scorns my person."

He cannot think that! Marianne let the page fall upon her lap. Surely he could not believe she was so inconstant, so untrustworthy! But what evidence had she given him otherwise? She could not trust him with the truth. At times she must resent him bitterly for all the grief he had caused her family.

She stretched out on the bed on her back, hands clasped behind her head. Instantly an image of a tall, lean frame leaped into her mind, and his eyes probed hers with a mixture of tenderness and suspicion. Why must her dearest friend be her most dreaded enemy as well?

The next thing Marianne knew, it was morning, and she had only a vague memory of having dreamed all night, restlessly, of the marquis staring at her in horror and stalking away, of him riding past and refusing even to look at her, of him entering a room and, upon seeing her, walking immediately out again.

At breakfast, Will showed her a letter he had drafted to her grandfather. A look at the dark circles under her cousin's eyes told Marianne he had stayed up late and slept as restlessly as she.

"My Dear Lord Marlow," the letter began. "I am pleased to say that Marianne is quite well and goes on magnificently with us.

119

However, there is an urgent matter concerning her that I must discuss with you in person. Unhappily, business matters prevent my leaving to report to you at your estate, and this is a matter of such delicacy as may not be entrusted in writing.

"If you think you may hazard a guess at the issue of which I speak, so much the better. You will understand why I request that you join us in London as soon as may be convenient so that we may talk privately.

"The come-out ball for your granddaughter Jane is in three days' time, as you may be aware. This may furnish an explanation for your repairing so hastily to town. It would be best if you did not reveal to anyone that you had received a letter from me or that I had spoken of a matter of urgency.

"I apologise for my lack of explicitness, but you will understand after we have a chance to talk. Your humble servant, William Sloan."

"Oh, Will, you have put the matter most excellently," Marianne said, toying with her devilled kidneys and settling at last for a bit of ham and some buttered toast with her coffee. "But you do not think he will take alarm, do you? I should not want him to come so rapidly that he had a carriage accident, or, heaven forbid, suffered the apoplexy."

Will sighed. "That was my concern also, Marianne, but while he has a considerable temper, I do not believe your grandfather is as rash as all that. I did assure him that you are well."

Celia joined them, looking far more refreshed than her husband, and the conversation became general while one of the maids brought fresh coffee. After her departure, Will handed Celia the letter and she perused it carefully.

"That is very fine," she said. "I believe it will serve."

"Will, Celia." Marianne hesitated, for the topic she was about to broach was painful to her, but she forced herself to continue. "Now that my mother is well cared for, and you know of her plight and may intervene for her if need be, do you not think I should return to Wiltshire?"

"Whatever for?" asked Will. "Now that I have asked your grandfather here, all the more reason you should stay." Celia nodded in agreement.

"What about Lord Whitestone?" Marianne asked. "He is sure to pursue the question of my identity and so may spoil everything. If I were not here—"

"He would bedevil the very life out of us to find out where you had gone," said Celia.

"He can scarcely come here morning, noon and night," Marianne pointed out. "I wish I could simply avoid him, but I cannot do so, for if I am in London I must attend Jane's ball, and she tells me Lord Whitestone has promised to come."

"You have been at balls with him before," said Will. "I cannot see that this will be any different."

"Perhaps not," said Marianne, "but I am very anxious. There is Priscilla Land, for one thing. She is the most terrible gossip, and she knows the Marlows are cousins to the Sloans, which Jer—Lord Whitestone apparently does not know. She will not hesitate to make mischief; that is her favourite occupation, I believe. Even without her, he surely must piece the puzzle together soon. He knows I am on the most intimate terms with Jane and Lucinda—oh, what if he were to guess the truth? He knows where Mother is, and he would have her thrown in prison before Jane's band had ceased playing!"

At this juncture, Miss Crane entered the room, although she customarily took tea and crumpets in her attic rooms.

"Pardon me, but I could not help but hear what you were saying." The elderly lady eyed a cold pigeon pie suspiciously but helped herself to bacon and eggs in napkins. "Where is the spirit of adventure I saw when first you arrived? You should not be quailing before his lordship like some milk-and-water miss! Why are you not dressing up as a footman this very moment, or selling gingerbread beneath his breakfast window? Remember how well your escapades stood you stead when that horrid Serena Brinoli —whose real name, I happen to know, is Martha Bowkes— forced you to confess to a lurid past, and he simply laughed. Do not give up so easily!"

It was amazing how much brighter the sunlight suddenly appeared, pouring through the chintz curtains. "You're right, of course," Marianne said. "Let Lord Whitestone look to his own reputation at Jane's come-out ball!"

121

═12═

THAT NIGHT WILL, having napped after luncheon, insisted on going with Marianne and Fritzella to visit Lady Mary. Celia offered to come as well, but it was decided that too large a group was not the thing and that further, she should remain home to throw Lord Whitestone off the scent should he call.

It seemed odd, Marianne reflected as their carriage creaked through the narrow streets, that the marquis had not returned that day to resume their interrupted conversation. Will had suggested going to the *Gazette* to check for news of spies, but to appear two days in a row might well arouse curiosity.

Marianne could see her cousin's concern as they halted in front of the modest row house, although no doubt he was more affected by the putrid smells and drunken revellers they had recently passed than by the inoffensive dwelling itself.

He stepped down and was permitted by Miss Crane to enter the vestibule, although the rules of the house forbade a man to penetrate further. Marianne hastened inside to prepare her mother.

Lady Mary, who had insisted on rising and dressing in anticipation of a visit despite Sarah and Elizabeth's exhortations to remain abed, looked healthier already. She had clearly eaten and rested better than in some time, and the lines of tension around her mouth had eased.

After they embraced, Marianne stepped back, still holding her mother's hands. "Mother, Will is here."

Lady Mary's face registered fear. "How did he . . Marianne, don't you remember . . ."

"I know, Mother, but Lord Whitestone escorted me home and

announced that my mother was here," Marianne explained. "Of course, he doesn't know who you are, but Will does."

"Then Lord Whitestone still doesn't suspect?" Lady Mary whispered.

Marianne shook her head. "I don't think so."

She guided her mother to the vestibule where, after a moment's hesitation, she and Will exchanged warm greetings. They were not well acquainted, Marianne had to remind herself, for it seemed as though two people who loomed so large in her life must naturally be on familiar terms. In fact, Lady Mary had seen Will only occasionally, and then generally in company, on previous occasions.

"I wanted to assure myself that you were well taken care of," Will said. "I have sent for your father."

"Do you mean you've told him everything?" Lady Mary appeared distressed. "It seems as if half of London must know by now."

"No, Mother, he's only sent a letter saying there's urgent business, but he hasn't explained what it is yet," Marianne said. "I think it's best Grandfather knows at this point, since Will and Celia are in on the secret."

Lady Mary sighed. "Have you told my brother?"

Will shook his head. "No. He's very angry with Lord Whitestone and I'm sure would take your part, but his wife is so concerned about her position in society, I had some misgivings that she might become hysterical."

Miss Crane popped in and then stuck her head out the front door, withdrawing it quickly. "Thought I heard hoofs," she said. "Wouldn't want Lord Whitestone to pay us a return visit, would we, not with Will's carriage out there plain as the moon in the sky."

"We'd better go." Marianne kissed her mother, and she and her companions set off a trifle nervously. However, no vengeful marquis appeared and they relaxed at last.

"I think I should write Jane and tell her I cannot attend her ball," said Marianne. "I do not mean to be overly timid, Miss Crane, but I am so very worried, I fear I will give myself away."

It was Will who disagreed. "We must all go on as normally as possible. After all, it could be a matter of mere days before the situation in France is resolved.''

''Or months,'' Marianne groaned.

Will frowned. ''I don't think so. If the Parisiennes refuse to surrender, what reason would your father have for remaining further?''

''How would he escape, while they're at war?'' countered Marianne sensibly. ''I keep thinking about it. Oh, I suppose you're right. I'm only torturing myself, and Jane will be sadly disappointed if I don't come. Very well, I shall go and force myself to flirt with Lord Whitestone as if nothing were wrong.''

''And perhaps pick up a bit of information that could be useful,'' added Miss Crane.

Jane looked delightful in her cherry silk dress trimmed with seed pearls. Lucinda, with unaccustomed modesty, wore a gown of pale pink. It was kind of her, Marianne thought, to take second place in costume to her sister on Jane's come-out.

''I am so excited I cannot bear it!'' cried Jane, whirling around the sisters' sitting room. ''Marianne, what time is it? It must be nine o'clock, it must!''

''It is only half past eight,'' said Lucinda sharply. ''Do be sensible, Jane. You will be exhausted before the evening has begun.''

''I told Mother we should have had a private dinner first,'' Jane babbled on. ''I simply cannot tolerate this waiting.''

''I could bear it well enough, were it not for your popping about like a Punch-and-Judy show,'' said Lucinda.

Marianne sighed. She herself wished the minutes were twice as long, and that the ball itself might somehow be avoided, but she knew that was an impossible dream. She had dressed in a yellow sarcenet gown embroidered in silver acorns, and Aunt Edith had said earlier the three girls looked like a bouquet of flowers. Still, it was odd to see Lucinda dressed so simply. Even her chestnut hair was plainly styled.

''It was thoughtful of you, Lucinda, to shade your own flame tonight,'' said Marianne.

''I beg your pardon?''

"You are dressed more simply than usual, no doubt to set your sister off to better advantage," she explained.

"That's true!" said Jane. "I am so overwrought, I hadn't noticed, Lucinda. Forgive me!"

"I cannot accept your praise, for I do not merit it," said Lucinda, and Marianne detected a strain in her voice. "I must confess I did not costume myself in this manner for Jane's benefit."

"Then why?" asked her cousin.

Lucinda heaved a deep sigh and stared down at the ivory fan in her lap. "I realize that Lord Whitestone no longer admires me, if indeed he ever did, for I think now perhaps it was a figment of my mother's imagination. Also, you see, these past two seasons, I have been quite discouraging to other gentlemen. I suppose it was my manner. I do tend to be rather snippish, don't I? There's no need to flatter me, I know it's true. I did not even want you to come to London, Marianne, for my own selfish reasons, and that sort of trait makes itself evident over time."

"I don't understand," Jane said.

"Do sit down and stop fidgeting," snapped Lucinda. When her sister obeyed, she continued. "I have driven off all the men who might have been my suitors, and would only make myself look foolish by parading about in the brightest colours and lowest-cut gowns, as Priscilla is wont to do."

"You can't mean you believe you would be slighted!" said Marianne.

"Not at a ball in my own home, of course; the men are bound to dance with me," said Lucinda. "But then everyone would gossip afterwards about what a fool I was and how I postured and put on airs, when everyone knows I'm next door to an apeleader."

"You're not an old maid at all," said Jane. "There's half a dozen men who admire you."

"All of whom have no fortune or no breeding and are totally ineligible," said Lucinda.

"What about Mr. Falmby?" asked Marianne.

"Who?"

"Mr. Falmby. I believe his first name is Frederick."

125

Lucinda frowned. "I cannot recall who you mean."

"He is meant to be a clergyman," said Marianne. "I have heard he has a good living awaiting him in Derbyshire. Good for a clergyman, of course, but he does come of noble family, and I believe he admires you."

"Oh, yes, he does!" cried Jane. "Do you not remember? He was at Vauxhall with that horrid Mr. Trimble, and you all but bit his head off, Lucinda. Yet when I apologised, he said I was too harsh toward you, and that you were quite right to take him down. Then he came to tea as well."

"Perhaps I do know who you mean," said Lucinda thoughtfully. "Will he be here tonight, do you think?"

"I do believe he will," said Jane. "You are not disgusted by him, are you, Lucinda? I should not like to see you wed a man you despised."

Lucinda briefly assumed an expression of patient martyrdom, then dropped it. "No, I shall not," she said. "If he can abide my sharp tongue, and is as eligible as you say, perhaps he will suit."

The time came at last for the girls to descend, and so they did, Lucinda graciously allowing her sister to precede her down the stairs to the ballroom. It had been decorated lavishly with wreaths of roses that set off Jane's dress, and bowers of green. Marianne was reminded of her first ball at the Hounsleys', and how she had slipped into the garden and met Lord Whitestone for the first time. How little she had suspected what heartbreak must come of that meeting, until Lucinda unwittingly revealed his identity.

The guests began to arrive, slowly at first and then in a great crush. It was evident that Jane's come-out was a huge success. Marianne, who did her best to make herself inconspicuous, was delighted to see her cousin sparkling and looking her best, and much sought after on the dance floor. Still, she seemed to Marianne to be gazing about for someone, and she suspected it was the not-yet-arrived Sir Edward.

Priscilla Land had arrived, however, in a clinging deep blue gown that emphasised the fairness of her hair and the well-formed shape of her figure. Nevertheless, the ranks of her admirers seemed to Marianne to be rather thin. Lucinda had apparently been correct. Beauty of face and form might dazzle for a season, but defects of character intruded thereafter, and a woman who had not a kind and pleasant disposition had best secure herself a mate as soon as possible.

And me? Marianne wondered. What will become of me when all this business comes out in the light of day? Even when her parents were cleared, there could be no question of a reconciliation between her and Lord Whitestone, not after she had humiliated him publicly and he had distressed her family in such a manner. She did not suppose she would ever find another man she could care for so deeply, but she must choose someone.

Determinedly, she stepped forth and was quickly asked to dance by a stoutish young gentleman. A quadrille followed, and a waltz, and a set of country dances, and one young man succeeded another, all of them equally polite and tedious.

At last Marianne saw the marquis enter, his tall figure unmistakable even across the packed ballroom. Quickly Priscilla attached herself to him, fanning herself rapidly as if she had been dancing to exhaustion, which she had not, and chattering gaily. Who would he marry when the time came for that? Marianne wondered. Whoever she was, she would be the luckiest of women.

She lost track of him in the crowd, but suddenly the marquis was bowing in front of her and asking for the next dance. Marianne consulted her card and saw that she had written a name upon it, but she could not for the life of her recall what the gentleman looked like and, as he did not appear to be in the offing, she accepted.

"You have not been much in evidence these past few days, my lord," she said as he led her out onto the floor.

"I have been much occupied," he said grimly. "I apologise for not being able to explain myself to you, Marianne, but these are matters of state."

"I quite understand, my lord," she said.

"You must call me Jeremy," he murmured as the band swept into a waltz.

"Yes . . . Jeremy," she said. The touch of his hand on her waist made her quiver, and they spoke no more for some minutes as they whirled about the floor. The music and background clatter of voices, the pastel colours of the gowns and the glow of hundreds of

127

candles merged in Marianne's mind. She felt light-headed, as if she had been drinking.

"You are most unnaturally silent," said his lordship. "Does something trouble you, my dear?"

The endearment burned through her like a draft of hot ale on a snowy night, and Marianne longed to pull him outside and be taken into his arms in earnest. But she must not, although this was surely the last time they would meet as friends, the last time he would ever speak her name.

"I fear I have worries of my own, which I also may not discuss," she said as lightly as she could. "But let us forget all this for tonight, shall we?"

He smiled and caught her hand even more tightly in his. "I think very shortly we should forget all our differences, should we not?"

The breath caught in her throat. Did he mean to propose marriage? Surely he would not be so foolish, not without determining her parentage and upbringing, even if he did not care for her dowry. What a horrible dilemma that would be, to have the man she loved offer for her, and to be forced to reveal a truth that would turn him away forever.

"I would like that very much," Marianne forced herself to answer. "But my lord . . . Jeremy. . . . It is possible that in a matter of days or perhaps weeks I shall be able to tell you why I have adopted these curious stratagems of mine, and then I fear you will be very angry with me."

"Nonsense," he said. "It cannot be so very serious." The music ended and they parted reluctantly as another man claimed her for the next dance.

It was some time before Marianne was able to go off by herself and catch her breath. Where was Jeremy? If they had only this one night left together, she wanted at least to speak to him again. Her fears of revealing more than she ought gave way before the longing to be near him, to hear his voice and be reassured that she still possessed his esteem.

Unable to locate him and feeling quite flushed with heat, Marianne stepped out onto the balcony. How romantic it would be to encounter him again in the moonlight! Perhaps he was thinking the same thing. On impulse, she dashed down the steps and into the garden.

Lanterns hung from the trees cast a faeryland spell over the scene as couples strolled arm in arm. Marianne gazed about her for a moment, then selected a likely-looking spot and walked toward it.

As she was about to push a screen of branches away and step into a small glade where she and her cousins had taken lemonade only a few days before, Marianne heard a low rumble of masculine voices and hesitated. Why should men be conversing among themselves in the garden during a ball?

"You are excessively single-minded, that is my opinion," said a rather nasal voice that, after searching her memory, Marianne identified tentatively as that of The Honourable Horace Trimble, the pear-shaped fool who, nevertheless, she reminded herself, held a post in the Foreign Office.

"I am forced to agree, Jeremy," said the voice of Sir Edward. "To suggest we spy on our fellow guests at a ball such as this is excessive."

"I thought we were agreed in advance," said Jeremy, subdued anger running through his tone. "Then I see the two of you making monkeys of yourselves over young ladies."

"You were not dancing with a certain Miss Sloan?" said Mr. Trimble.

"One is allowed a certain degree of discretion," said Lord Whitestone stiffly. "Clearly I cannot spend all evening lurking about the card room and engaging other gentlemen in conversation."

"Nor can we," said Sir Edward sensibly. "It is most unfair of you to insist we pass a social evening in work, Jeremy. I gravely doubt we shall catch any French spies here."

"Have you no memory, man?" demanded his friend. "We have in our hands a signed confession testifying that treason is spread even in the highest circles of government!"

"Surely one night can make no difference," Ned protested.

"One night at this juncture can make a very large difference indeed," the marquis answered. "Napoleon becomes desperate. We know that someone, most likely an assassin, has been smuggled into London. We must learn his whereabouts and his target!"

"Forgive me, my lord, but I fear you go too far," said Mr. Trimble. "Our spy did not, did he, mention more than that such a plot had been suggested. Only suggested, not planned."

"But he said Arnet is one of the leaders in Paris now, and we all know him to have connexions yet in London," Lord Whitestone pressed on urgently. "There is another aspect to this which causes me even graver concern."

"Something you have not imparted to us?" Ned asked.

"My suspicions have only just come together tonight, on seeing how closely gentlemen may be watched and how little ladies are," said his lordship. "Do you not recall some mention that Arnet had sent his wife south, for her health?"

"I believe he said something of that," said Mr. Trimble. "But he knew no more details of that than of the traitors in our own government. What do you make of it?"

"Madame Arnet is an Englishwoman," said the marquis. "She would not be distinguished here by her accent, would she?"

"She would be recognised!" protested Sir Edward. "She could not come waltzing into a ball at her own brother's house and think to escape detection."

"I did not mean that she was here," Jeremy said irritably. "But she might go about London more or less unnoticed. She might have spoken with ladies, gentlemen, obtained information, without anyone becoming suspicious."

"So we are to spend the evening looking for a lady who isn't there?" said Mr. Trimble. "Poppycock!"

"Listen, my friend," snapped Lord Whitestone. "The life of our prince or our prime minister may be at stake. We must listen and question unobtrusively. Has anyone been asked about these gentlemen's habits—when they ride in the park, where they dine? Has anyone encountered an unknown lady recently?"

"Why, you have done," chortled Ned. "Your little friend Marianne is quite a mystery, is she not?"

Marianne felt her heart stick in her throat and tightened her grip on the tree branch to keep herself from swaying. Surely he must deduce the truth now!

"She is not near old enough," the marquis said, dismissing the comment. "Furthermore, you know perfectly well she could not be mixed up in such a business as this."

"It was only meant as a jest," said his friend.

"Are we agreed then?" asked the marquis. "We shall be diligent tonight—all of us, Mr. Trimble—for I will wager this: With almost all of the *ton* present in this house tonight, it is almost certain that at least one person knows the whereabouts of Madame Arnet, or whoever this person is who has come to London."

Perceiving that the gentlemen were about to break up their conversation and not wishing to be caught eavesdropping, Marianne carefully let go of the branch and stepped back.

She turned to find herself face to face with the fair-haired, fox-eyed Priscilla Land.

=13=

"WELL, WELL," SAID Priscilla, words that in her mouth had the effect of accusing one of all manner of wrongdoing and finding one guilty at the same time.

"Oh, hello, Priscilla," said Marianne breathlessly. "Looking for someone?"

"Merely taking the air." Priscilla fanned herself. "And you?"

"The same." Marianne hesitated, unsure whether the better course were to retreat as fast as possible or to remain where she was. She suspected that Priscilla had been following her and decided that fleeing could only rouse suspicion. Further, Priscilla would be sure to tell the men that Marianne had been there, in any case.

"Something I've been meaning to ask you," said Priscilla. "I seem to recall being about to mention in Lord Whitestone's presence that you and Lucinda were cousins, and the both of you all but shouted me down. Why was that?"

After a moment of near-panic, Marianne managed to say with simulated ease, "Oh, did we? I do not recall it, Miss Land. I'm certain you must have mistaken our intention."

"Indeed?" Unfortunately, it was at that moment that the marquis himself all but collided with them as he exited the glade. "Lord Whitestone! Tell me, were you aware that Miss Sloan was cousins with Jane and Lucinda?"

He looked puzzled. "No, I was not. The mystery grows, does it not, Marianne? How did you know this, Miss Land?"

Irked at being addressed so formally when Marianne was called by her Christian name, Priscilla shrugged and said haughtily, "Everyone knows that the Sloans and the Marlows are cousins. Therefore, Will Sloan's sister must be Lucinda and Jane's cousin."

"But she isn't—" Lord Whitestone stopped. "Or perhaps she is. If you will excuse me, ladies?" Marianne released a sigh of relief as he stepped away.

"There is something smoky about all this, Miss Sloan, and I mean to get to the bottom of it—Oh, hello, Sir Edward!"

Marianne ducked away and left Priscilla simpering at the baronet. She had barely reentered the ballroom when Lucinda caught her by the arm. "Marianne, you will never guess what has happened! Something positively awful!"

For a moment, she couldn't swallow. However, before her silence became embarrassing, her cousin hurried on. "It's Grandfather! He's arrived, just like that, without a word to anyone!"

"Didn't Will tell you?" As soon as she said the words, Marianne realised that of course he had not. Will had chosen not to enlighten the Marlows and so it would have been awkward to explain that Lord Marlow had been sent for.

"Tell me what?" gasped Lucinda.

"He—he had some matter of urgent business to discuss with Grandfather," said Marianne weakly. "He asked him to come."

"Why should he arrive tonight, in the midst of everything?" Lucinda was clearly trying to avert hysteria. "You know how he feels about Lord Whitestone. I'm terrified that he'll make a scene, that he'll . . . well, you know. He's off in the library with Will and Father now, and heaven knows what they're talking about. Do you?"

After a brief hesitation, Marianne nodded. "Yes, I do. It has to do with my parents, Lucinda. I'm afraid that's all I can tell you now. Is Jane upset?"

"Hardly," Lucinda said more calmly. "You would think she'd be in a tizzy, wouldn't you, it being her come-out, and her whole future riding on it, but no, she thinks it's splendid. I've no doubt she'd quite enjoy a row. That quiet sister of mine is becoming something entirely different."

"She always was," said Marianne, steering her cousin toward a secluded corner and feeling grateful that the conversation had been turned so easily. "Have you seen Mr. Falmby?"

"Yes." Lucinda smiled. "I had not liked him at first. I thought him high in the instep and quite a dullard, but now I believe that's just a manner he adopts with strangers. He's been most attentive tonight and, as you surmised, he is entirely eligible.''

"There's been no one else?'' Marianne asked. "You needn't resolve upon marrying one man simply because of a single evening.''

"I knew what I was saying.'' Lucinda gazed out at the dancing swirl and it occurred to Marianne that the older girl was maturing. "Have you noticed Priscilla Land tonight? She's not precisely inundated, is she?''

"She was out in the garden, sneaking about in pursuit of Lord Whitestone, if you want my opinion,'' said Marianne.

"What were you doing out in the garden?''

Marianne winked. "Spying,'' she said.

Lucinda rapped her shoulder with her fan. "Don't even breathe that word!'' she whispered urgently. "Don't you know—it's on everyone's lips—they've caught a French spy at the Foreign Office, and he's confessed all manner of things. Even about your father, if you'll forgive my mentioning it.''

"What did he say about him?''

"That he is a great leader in Paris, one of Napoleon's most trusted supporters, that sort of thing,'' said Lucinda. "It does make matters even worse, doesn't it?''

Marianne bit her lip. Perhaps this wasn't such a propitious time for Grandfather to arrive, after all.

She glanced up and saw that Lord Marlow, Will, and Uncle Charles had rejoined the gathering. With a speaking look at Lucinda, she squared her shoulders and headed through the crowd, her cousin trailing behind.

Marianne was halfway to her grandfather when Lord Whitestone intervened. "There you are,'' he said. "I have been looking for you. Don't you recall that you promised me this dance?''

Seeing her grandfather staring at them, Marianne felt herself growing flustered. "I don't . . . did I really? No, you're teasing me.''

"You did indeed.'' With that, the marquis swept her into a quadrille. During it, happily, the presence of the others in their set kept conversation at a discreet level.

Nevertheless, Lord Whitestone managed to murmur, "Were

you avoiding me, then? I fail to understand you, Marianne. Perhaps you enjoy these pretenses of yours. I don't wish to intrude upon you."

She thought of his letter, and was certain his doubts had been renewed. Oh, dear, one moment he verged on proposing matrimony and the next he supposed himself unwelcome even as a dancing partner. "I don't enjoy this pretense at all . . . Jeremy," she said firmly. "You're not intruding. It's only that someone has arrived whom I wished to greet."

The marquis looked across the room. "Lord Marlow?" he said. "Is he truly your grandfather, Marianne? I can't imagine him countenancing such odd behaviour in one of his granddaughters."

"I can't either," she agreed. "Shall I be cast out in disgrace, do you think? Would you give me shelter?" She hoped she had turned his thoughts in another direction, for the moment, at least.

"The shelter of my arms, most assuredly." He smiled warmly and some of Marianne's tension ebbed.

At last the dance ended and she crossed the room to where the Earl of Marlow stood, an imposingly regal figure in his tan breeches and old-fashioned powdered wig.

"Grandfather!" She stood on tiptoe and kissed his cheek. "I am so glad to see you."

"Indeed, my dear," he said gruffly. "I was surprised to see you dancing with a certain gentleman."

Marianne glanced about, but only Will and Celia stood near. "I fear I have been thrown much into his company," she said.

Jane came scampering up to Lord Marlow. "I thought you would remain closeted forever! How very happy I am to have you here at my come-out!"

"Yes, it is my pleasure also," he said. "Of course by rights it should be a come-out for both my granddaughters."

"Indeed it should!" said Jane. "You have only to say the word and we shall announce that it is."

"Jane!" protested Lucinda, joining them. "You cannot mean that! Not after all we have . . . all Marianne has been through to protect us!"

"Don't you see?" Jane pulled the little group into a corner where no one was likely to approach. "Her plan has worked!

Haven't you seen how he's favoured her, danced with her twice tonight, made it evident to everyone that his affections are well-nigh fixed?''

Lucinda stared at her with a stunned look. ''That was what I planned,'' Marianne admitted. ''But, Jane, you can't mean to torment him with his feelings. I never thought it would truly come to that.''

''Would someone be so kind as to explain to me what you are discussing?'' said their grandfather. ''I believe I have missed some point or other.''

''I'm sorry. I forget you didn't know,'' said Jane. ''After Marianne found herself thrust into an acquaintance with a certain gentleman, she resolved that she must either cower in her room or be bold, and so she was.''

''Not too bold, I hope?'' Lord Marlow raised an eyebrow. Marianne wished fervently that Jane would sink through the floor and never finish this particular conversation, for she sensed a storm brewing.

''Not at all!'' Jane went on blithely. ''You should have seen her dressed as a gypsy.''

''A gypsy?''

''Yes. She told our fortunes at Vauxhall, or rather, Madame Cransky did. That's Miss Crane, Celia's old nurse. Then Marianne dressed up as a parlourmaid and spilled the tea in Lord Whitestone's lap.''

''Surely she's jesting,'' Lord Marlow said, turning to Marianne. She shook her head reluctantly. ''I'm afraid not,'' she said. ''I thought that if I could intrigue Lord Whitestone, I could win his admiration. If all of London were to see it, then when the truth came out, it would be he who was humiliated and had to slink off to the country.''

''Will!'' Grandfather bellowed, and that young man approached with uncharacteristic timidity. ''Surely you did not give your consent to Marianne's dashing about dressed as a gypsy?''

He looked sheepish. ''I'm afraid I did, my lord,'' he said. ''It seemed a harmless idea.''

''Harmless? My granddaughter? Where is that blasted Lord Whitestone? It's due to him my own daughter's hiding out with

". . . with . . . I cannot even say the word in polite company! And the bravest man who ever served England is in peril of his life, and my own flesh and blood is reduced to posing as a gypsy and can't even have her own come-out ball!"

"No, Grandfather, please," Marianne said, vaguely aware that her two cousins were standing openmouthed at this speech. "Let's talk this over calmly, after the party."

He wavered and appeared to be thinking the better of his plan. All might have gone well then had it not been for the odious Mr. Trimble.

He sauntered up to the little group and insinuated himself into the conversation with all the grace of a weasel attempting to frolic inconspicuously among a band of rabbits.

"How very pleasant to see you here, your lordship," he said after introductions had been made. "I hope nothing is amiss? Is there some matter of urgency that has required your presence in London?"

"Does not my granddaughter's come-out ball present reason enough?" said the earl edgily.

"Indeed, indeed," said Mr. Trimble. "I was merely wondering—well, there is the matter of that other granddaughter of yours."

"Lucinda has been out since two seasons ago."

"Come, my lord! I think you understand me." Mr. Trimble drew from his waistcoat pocket a snuffbox shaped like a lady's leg, withdrew a quantity of the white powder, placed it on his handkerchief, and inserted it into his nose. Marianne had always found snuff-taking repulsive, and to do so without apology in the presence of ladies struck her as ill-mannered indeed, even insulting.

"I fear I do not understand you," Lord Marlow said. "To whom do you refer, Mr. Trimble?"

The pear-shaped fellow sneezed mightily and then said, "Why, to Miss Arnet, of course."

"Why do you refer to her?"

"You must know that there is talk about town that her parents are, shall we say, still active among the enemy. I merely meant that it is unfortunate that she must therefore be deprived of her season in London."

"She is not deprived because of any actions her parents may have taken," said the earl with growing annoyance. "It is the actions of someone quite different that are at fault."

"I suppose I see what you mean."

Mr. Trimble paused, and Marianne, having overheard the conversation in the garden, supposed his whole purpose in intruding upon them was to sniff about for any clue as to her mother's location. Surely even such a toplofty fop as Mr. Trimble must see by now that he was offensive and that the Arnets' own family was the least likely of anyone to give her away.

Yet apparently that truth had not reached the small brain nestled in the swollen expanse of his head. "Nevertheless," he went on, "we are all patriotic Englishmen here, and no one would wish to protect a traitor, now, would they?"

At this point, seeing her grandfather about to explode and ruin the entire scheme, Lucinda seized Mr. Trimble firmly by the elbow and jerked backwards, throwing him off balance. He stumbled, and as he did she pushed him about and gave him a shove that sent him staggering into a drunken duke, so that both of them landed on the floor.

"Good gracious!" It was Aunt Edith, materialised at last and come to help her eldest daughter. Quickly the two of them dusted off the victims and spirited them away to the punch table.

"What an insufferable boor the man is!" said Lord Marlow. "Imagine speaking in that manner of two of the finest people—"

"But he does not know, and he must not," said Marianne. "Think, Grandfather! You may endanger them both with your hot temper."

The earl nodded. "I suppose I'd best have some claret and find myself a comfortable spot to sit." Marianne watched anxiously as he and Will moved off together. A moment later, surrounded by her aunt and two cousins, she quickly explained the true situation of her parents.

All seemed to be going well again until she observed the despised Mr. Trimble approaching her grandfather and bowing to him, making some sort of apology, it appeared. The situation was volatile, and she hurried over in time to hear his words.

"I fear I overstepped myself," Mr. Trimble was saying as he bowed. "Pray forgive me, your lordship. You see, I had been asked to chat up anyone who might have any information as to the whereabouts of certain persons believed to have come to London recently."

"And who might that be?"

"Why, your daughter, sir."

"The deuce you say! What is this nonsense about her being in London?"

"It's mere conjecture, no doubt, no doubt at all," babbled Mr. Trimble. "It was Lord Whitestone who brought the matter up. It's him that's suspicious of everyone, sees a French spy under every table."

"You don't mean to tell me that Lord Whitestone has instructed you to spy at my granddaughter's come-out ball, in my own home?"

Marianne looked about for a weapon, anything to smite Mr. Trimble with. A pox on the man for all the trouble he'd caused, and now he was inflaming Grandfather further. But her eye fell on nothing but a branch of candles, and even she dared not set fire to Mr. Trimble.

"In a manner of speaking, yes," that loathsome person continued. "He did ask me and Sir Edward Beamish to scout about, if you will, ask a few questions here and there. He's of the opinion that Madame Arnet has returned to assassinate the prime minister, you see."

"To do what?" Lord Marlow's voice had risen to a roar. Unfortunately, the band was taking an interval between dances, so the sound carried to the far reaches of the ballroom, and everyone turned to see what had caused the commotion. Marianne glimpsed her aunt bustling toward them. Too late, she thought.

Lord Whitestone arrived first. "Is there some problem?" he inquired. "Perhaps I may be of assistance."

"I do not need a young whippersnapper like you to lend me assistance in my own home!" bellowed the earl. "And I'll thank you not to set your scurvy acquaintances spying on me at my granddaughter's come-out ball!"

139

The marquis paled ever so slightly, and cast a shrivelling look upon Mr. Trimble, who mumbled his way backwards until he collided with a large and quite solid pedestal.

"I fear I have been misrepresented," Lord Whitestone said quietly.

"Misrepresented?" roared the earl, and now all of the ballroom was listening in earnest. Marianne had a fleeting image of giant ears blooming up from the heads of London's finest ladies and gentlemen. "I have in your own hand, in a letter addressed to me, that you forbid me to introduce my granddaughter to London society, that you will cause me and all those I love to be shunned if she so much as sets foot among the *ton*. Do you deny it?"

"No, I do not," said the marquis, his voice steady although Marianne saw the muscles tighten in his jaw. "But I do not believe this is the proper place to speak of this matter, Lord Marlow."

"Damn if it ain't!" Grandfather was in full tilt now, and Marianne, although she was praying silently that he might somehow come to his senses, had a distressing feeling that there was to be no stopping him.

"Jonas, please!" Edith had reached him at last and caught at his elbow. "Think of what a commotion you're making! Think of Jane! Think of Lucinda!"

"Are they to be scorned and pushed aside too, if this young coxcomb finds something objectionable in their ancestry?" cried Lord Marlow. "Is every lady in London subject to this arrogant fool's whims, his misplaced patriotism and inflated sense of his own worth?"

"You have gone too far, sir," Lord Whitestone said tightly. "I must ask that you cease these calumnies immediately."

"Or what?" challenged Grandfather. "Or you will leave this house? I invite you to do so."

Several of the onlookers gasped. The insult was an open one, and, had it not been for Lord Marlow's advanced age, Lord Whitestone would have been obligated to call him out, despite the illegality of dueling.

"I shall accept your offer gladly," said the marquis. "However, there is one thing I will say first."

"Say it then!"

"That you defend your family is understandable. But even now, our country is locked in a deadly battle with one of the greatest fiends the world has ever known. One of the men closest to him, one of his most influential aides, is your son-in-law, this girl's father. I have reason to believe she knows a great deal more of his movements than you might surmise, in your partiality. I believe the lives of some of England's greatest men may be in danger as a result of her treachery."

"Nonsense!" cried Lord Marlow. "You make yourself ridiculous in the eyes of this very assembly! Treachery indeed! Did I not with my own eyes see you dancing with her but a few minutes ago?"

The words were out. Marianne stood numbly, the astonished murmurs of the crowd behind her seeming very distant indeed. Much louder, she heard a humming in her ears, the rushing of the blood through her veins. It had been said. There was nowhere to flee, no more disguises to hide behind, no more clever words to turn the marquis's thoughts.

"I fail to understand you, Lord Marlow," said Jeremy, a touch of uncertainty in his voice. Dimly, Marianne perceived Sir Edward Beamish standing alongside him, mirroring his confusion.

"My granddaughter!" The earl's voice must surely have carried halfway to Wiltshire. "Marianne Arnet!"

There was nothing for Marianne to do but stand there and watch as the marquis turned a disbelieving countenance in her direction. The entire room was silent, shocked into an unaccustomed stillness as he stared at her from no more than thirty feet away.

In her most horrible nightmares, she had never dreamed that the unmasking would come so publicly or be so humiliating to them both. Before such an audience, there could be no attempts at explanation, no chance for him to question her or tell her if he now doubted the truth of his suspicions. She saw emotions flash across his face—incredulity, anger, doubt, betrayal—in the brief moment before he turned and strode away, Sir Edward hurrying behind him.

"There," said Grandfather. "Now let us have some music.

Play!'' There was a brief rustling as the musicians resumed their positions on the platform, and then the sound of a country dance once again filled the ballroom.

As the people moved away and resumed the customary dance of polite society, the clattering of tongues took up this new and fascinating revelation, this deliciously scandalous scene. Marianne stood unmoving until Jane took her arm.

"Oh, Marianne, I am sorry," said her cousin. "I'm not sorry Grandfather got angry and I'm not sorry he told the truth, but I'm sorry for you. You had rather come to care for him, hadn't you?"

"It doesn't matter," Marianne said tonelessly. "It would have happened sooner or later."

Her family was closing round—Lucinda, Uncle Charles, the Sloans—all of them stunned as well, except Edith, who was near hysteria.

"He has ruined us!" she moaned. "I cannot believe it. No, Charles, do not contradict me. I do not question that your father had the highest of motives, but it is not you who have worked so hard to build a reputation for your daughters and to see that they have the finest gowns and are invited to the best homes. You will not be slighted by your friends, nor excluded from their activities. But I shall be, and my poor Jane and Lucinda."

To Marianne's surprise, Lucinda spoke back to her mother in a grave voice. "I fear you are mistaken, mother," she said. "Our friends will not cut us, but our acquaintances will. I lived in fear that such a thing as this would transpire, just as you did, but now I find I am of a different mind altogether. Lord Whitestone's behaviour was abominable. He has insulted this family and attempted to spy on us in our home."

"I'm afraid this was partly my fault," said Will before Edith could chastise her daughter. "I'm the one who gave Marianne permission to run about dressed in costumes. I never thought about the more subtle consequences, only whether she might be attacked in the street. Now I see that I endangered her character, and quite rightly infuriated Lord Marlow and . . . something far worse."

"What is that?" asked Grandfather, joining the little cluster.

"I fear that by allowing them to be in proximity to each other, I may have . . . I may have allowed Marianne's affections to be engaged.''

"Engaged?'' snapped the earl. "Engaged to whom?''

"You misunderstand!'' cried Edith. "She is not engaged. He merely means that—''

"Mother, please!'' Jane stopped them with an upraised hand. "You are creating an uproar and making this whole scandal even worse than it is. Do you not see how everyone is staring at us? It is my ball and I shall give the orders. You, Will, are to dance with Lucinda immediately, and Grandfather with Mother, and Father with Celia. I shall escort Marianne upstairs and see that she is well taken care of. Not a word of argument! Go on, all of you.''

Their mouths open in astonishment at this tirade by the usually shy Jane, the family did as she had commanded. Marianne allowed herself to be led up the stairs to Jane's room, feeling all the while as if she had borrowed an unfamiliar body.

"And while I am giving orders, you, Marianne, are to lie down and rest yourself,'' said Jane kindly. "I shall summon the maid immediately, and you are to borrow any of my nightgowns you like.''

"Don't send anyone, please,'' Marianne said. "I'd rather be alone if you don't mind.''

"Of course.'' Jane sat beside her on the bed and slipped an arm about her waist. "Marianne, please don't feel that no one can understand what you're going through. Ned Beamish is gone as well, you know.''

"I hadn't thought . . .'' Marianne paused. Sir Edward had been paying Jane marked attention these past days, and her cousin had responded with a sparkling happiness that was new to her. "He will be back, I'm sure of it.''

"I wish I could be so certain as you are.''

"It will all come out sooner or later about my parents, and if Sir Edward hasn't reconsidered himself before then, he'll certainly come round to make his apologies,'' said Marianne.

"Surely Lord Whitestone will do the same.''

"No.'' Marianne stared down at her hands and fought back the tears. "No, he won't, Jane. I've deceived him and made a fool of him publicly. How can he ever forgive me? How can I forgive him for having increased my parents' jeopardy through his blind prejudice, and insulted my family, and hurt all of the rest of you?''

"Is your own pain of no account?"

"Don't mind that, Jane, I shall recover." Marianne spoke with as much assurance as she could muster. Finally her cousin departed reluctantly to see to her guests.

But she would never get over it, Marianne thought. There could never be a man she would love so deeply or so hopelessly. Perhaps eventually she might make an agreeable union with someone tolerable who would treat her well and whom she could respect, but she would never again be held in Jeremy's arms, never see his dear face so close to hers.

The tears slipped unchecked down her cheeks, and Marianne sank down on the bed hopelessly. It would never come right. How could he be so pigheaded, so unwilling even to consider that Father and Mother . . .

Mother. The tears stopped abruptly. Mother! Lord Whitestone had been introduced to her as Marianne's mother, and he knew where she was. It was only a matter of time—perhaps it was already too late—before he recovered enough from his anger to realise the truth. He would seize Lady Mary and haul her off to prison, where in her weakened state she would surely die. Marianne knew her mother would rather perish than endanger her husband by revealing the truth.

She sat up, fists clenched. She must get Will and Uncle Charles—Then she remembered the crush of carriages outside. They would never get clear in time to catch up with Lord Whitestone. Then there would be arguments and discussions as to who should go, and how they should get there, and every minute would add to Mary Arnet's deadly peril.

There could be no question about it. She must go herself, alone, to warn her mother.

=14=

THERE WAS NO time even to change her embroidered yellow sarcenet gown for something more suitable. Marianne fetched her velvet cloak from the wardrobe and darted out into the hall and down the back staircase.

She saw several servants but they did not notice her in their haste to set up the tables for supper. She slipped out the back and down a darkened side of the garden, through the gate to the cobbled mews where the stables were situated.

As she paused for breath, Marianne gazed about wildly. The sound of her running feet had drawn a groom, and he stared at her in surprise until they recognised each other at the same instant. He had worked on Grandfather's estate the previous year before coming to the Marlow town house.

"Miss Arnet!" he said. "What be you doing here at this hour?"

His name came to her. "Arthur, please don't ask questions. It's a terrible emergency," she gasped. "You must saddle me a horse, at once! Please. Oh, it's urgent!"

His face reflected doubt, but he had not been raised to disobey the ladies and gentlemen of the household. After a moment's hesitation, during which Marianne thought her heart would stop beating altogether, he nodded and disappeared into the stable.

An eon later, he returned, leading a spirited little mare that Marianne recognised as Jane's horse, Ginger. She swore silently to take good care of it and to send some money round for Arthur later, since she had brought none with her. Were it not for that, she might have taken a hackney, but that was of no importance now.

Marianne was grateful for his help in handing her up into the sidesaddle, for ball gowns were not meant for riding and she knew hers was being sadly crushed. She felt a momentary pang, for the dress had cost more than enough to keep a labourer's family for a year. But what did that signify beside her mother's life?

Once settled firmly atop Ginger, Marianne urged the horse forward and they were off. She concentrated on getting past the crush of carriages, which was not difficult except for the stares she drew from idle grooms and footmen. Then she was galloping through the dark and shadowy streets of London, the flickering oil lamps serving more to add eery, wavering shapes than to light her way. She wished the more brilliant gas lights had been installed in all of London, but as yet they were found in only a few parishes.

The fashionable streets of Mayfair soon yielded to a narrow tangle, and a bird of fear fluttered in Marianne's throat. She had thought that by now she could easily find her way to Miss Crane's little house, but she had never ridden there alone. In the darkness and her near-panic, she became disoriented.

She must not lose heart, she ordered herself. Lord Whitestone might not think of her mother until morning. Even now he might be lying in the arms of Serena Brinoli, but that was a poor consolation, she had to admit.

At last Marianne recognised a shop, and turned herself about. Gradually she saw more and more familiar landmarks in the twisted streets. She kicked Ginger forward as a group of men called and whistled to her outside a tavern, and tried not to think what an odd picture she must make in her shimmering ball gown, with her hair flying disorderly about her face as she rode through the streets.

A thin drizzle began to fall and Marianne shivered. She would likely catch cold, but that was of little importance. Yet what of her mother, riding away in this rain after she was warned? Curse Lord Whitestone for all he had put them through! How dare her heart play traitor to her, when he deserved only her hatred?

She reached Boar's Lane and paused, looking down it and feeling relief wash over her at seeing no one astir. There were no shouting Bow Street Runners, no furious Lord Whitestone battering at the door. Nor, listen as she might, could Marianne hear anything save faint voices from inside the buildings, and the growing patter of the rain.

She hastened forward and drew to a halt in front of the house. Ginger was quickly tied to a post, and Marianne pounded on the door.

When no one came, a dry terror crept up her throat. All within had been arrested and carried off this half hour past. Or perhaps Lady Mary had died of her illness that very afternoon . . . No! She beat upon the door again and at last heard noises within.

The door opened a crack and Sarah's thin, anxious face looked out. "Oh, it's only you, Miss," she said, opening the door wider and hurrying Marianne inside. "Whatever be you doing out on such a night? Look at your gown! Why, it's fair ruined! Whatever is wrong?"

"Is my mother here?" Marianne asked.

"Why, yes, but she's in bed this hour or more," said Sarah. "Miss Crane says we're not to disturb her."

"Is she here? Miss Crane?" Marianne shivered with unexpected hope.

"Yes, Miss, she's in the parlour with Elizabeth," said Sarah. "Come in, won't you?"

Marianne hurried in the direction she indicated and burst into the small, cozy parlour where Fritzella and Elizabeth sat with their feet up on stools, drinking tea.

"Good heavens, child!" said Miss Crane. "What a sight you are. What are you doing here—foolish question. Forgive me. You've urgent news, haven't you?"

Marianne nodded tensely and forced herself not to think about how desperately her body longed to sink before the crackling fire. "It's Mother. Lord Whitestone knows. About me, I mean. Grandfather was so angry . . . at the ball. . . . he—he shouted it out. It was horrible, but never mind that. Any minute now Jer—Lord Whitestone is going to remember about my mother, and put two and two together, and then they'll come for her."

Sarah and Elizabeth were staring at her curiously, but neither of them asked anything. It struck Marianne fleetingly how very different their lives had been from hers, that they accepted with only

147

mild curiosity that someone should be in trouble with the law and might need to flee unexpectedly in the middle of the night.

Miss Crane swung into action. "Elizabeth," she said, "go upstairs and get Mary dressed at once. Sarah, summon Rob. Send him for a hackney. We can't ride in the rain and furthermore we'd be recognised." The two women jumped to obey.

"Where are you taking her?" asked Marianne.

"That does present a bit of a problem, doesn't it?" Fritzella rubbed her hands together speculatively. "What a pity it's such a bad night. We don't dare keep her outside for long. Well, there's no helping it. We'll take her to the Sloans' house and smuggle her into my rooms."

"Are you sure that's wise?" asked Marianne. "They would search there, surely."

"Not tonight," Miss Crane said. "One doesn't burst into the house of gentlefolk without the proper papers, even Lord Whitestone, and he'll not get those tonight. Also, I doubt he'll expect anything so rash of us."

"What about tomorrow? If they find her—"

"Nonsense." Miss Crane radiated confidence. "By then your grandfather will spirit her off somewhere. To an inn, perhaps, or the house of an old friend."

In her exhausted and dampened state, Marianne could see only obstacles, each looming like a great vicious bear. "But she's so ill . . ."

"It's only for a little while," soothed her friend. "This business in France can't go on much longer."

Sarah and Elizabeth returned, bundling Lady Mary between them. She embraced Marianne, who quickly explained the situation.

"Now we're off," said Miss Crane. "Come along, Marianne."

"I can't," she said. "I suppose we could lead Ginger, but what will everyone think when they go upstairs and find I've gone?"

"We'll send a messenger."

"To say what? Miss Crane, don't you see, we must tell no one what we're doing, not even the Sloans' servants."

"Be we nobody?" inquired Sarah a bit huffily.

"That's not what I meant," said Marianne. "We trust *you*." The other woman smiled, mollified. "Oh, Miss Crane, I do want to rest a bit, and then I promise I'll borrow some heavy cloak, and when the rain lets up a bit I'll find my way back."

"Too dangerous," said Miss Crane. "I'll have Rob stay and he can drive back alongside you, at least until you're within sight of Marlow House. Well enough?"

"That sounds wonderful," said Marianne, and sank gratefully onto the sofa.

Within minutes after Lady Mary and Miss Crane departed, the house was restored to restful quiet. Elizabeth went up to bed and Sarah, after a few minutes' indecision, apparently realised Marianne was not to become a vivacious companion and followed Elizabeth's example.

Alone before the fire, Marianne allowed herself to give in briefly to her weariness. She had never been so frightened and worried in her life, but now it was over. Her mother was safe and warm in Miss Crane's capable hands and soon she would be under Will's protection.

A pounding at the door startled Marianne so that she nearly dropped her cup of tea. She leaped to her feet, thinking that Miss Crane had surely come back to retrieve something, until she remembered that of course Fritzella would have a key to the house. It might be Rob, but he would scarcely pound so.

Then she heard a man's voice cry, "Open up! Open up in the name of the crown!"

Marianne caught the edge of the sofa to steady herself. They had come so quickly. They might even have passed the hackney in the night. Had she paused for an instant to summon aid at Marlow House, or had she lost her way any more thoroughly, her mother would still be here, trapped.

No one responded from upstairs, and Marianne made her way slowly toward the door, dreading what she would find when she opened it. There was no help for it; if she did not come, they would smash the door down, and where was the sense of that?

Arranging her ruined cloak so as to hide as much of her damaged gown as possible, she opened the door.

She found herself staring into the heartless pale eyes of a red-coated officer. "We're here to arrest a traitor to the crown," he snapped. "Yield up Madame Arnet or we shall haul the lot of you off to Newgate."

Marianne looked past him into the wet street and saw several dozen soldiers waiting in the mist and, behind them, mounted on a fiery stallion, an erect figure that sent a stab of pain through her heart.

"My mother is not here," she said. "I have come ahead of you and warned her, sir, and if you wish to pack me off to prison, you may do so now."

The officer hesitated, then found his voice again. "We must search the house," he barked.

Marianne heard footsteps behind her and then Elizabeth's voice said, "This way, sir."

Marianne stood outside, huddling into her cloak, as the soldiers prowled through the house. She heard their footsteps upstairs, like lead-footed mice, poking into every corner. They searched the attic and the cellar and the alley in back before gathering once more in the street.

"I order you to accompany us to prison, unless you will reveal here and now the whereabouts of Madame Arnet," the officer ordered her.

"I will not," Marianne said. She felt chilled through her bones, both from her damp clothing and from the thought of being cast into a dank and forbidding prison. Surely her family would find her soon enough, but even they could not free her until the truth could be told. Heaven knew when that might be.

She looked up as Lord Whitestone approached on his horse. After a tense moment, the marquis turned to the officer. "Captain Martin, I will take responsibility for this young woman. She is the granddaughter of the Earl of Marlow and I do not believe any good will be accomplished by placing her in prison."

"But my lord, she's aiding and abetting this traitor, this assassin!"

"I have, as it turns out, once seen this Madame Arnet with my own eyes, and I do not believe it is she personally who would attack our leaders, although no doubt she is in league with the scoundrels," said the marquis. "I suggest you have your men fan out and search the streets, for she cannot have gone far."

"Very good, sir," said the officer, and snapped orders to his men, who quickly dispersed. They left Marianne and the marquis facing each other from a distance of perhaps a dozen feet that might as well have been a million miles.

"Come in, Miss Marianne," said Elizabeth's voice behind her. "Mayhap it stopped raining, but it's powerful damp out there."

"In a minute, Elizabeth," she said, unable to turn her eyes from the sight of Jeremy, his eyes cold, his hard body tensed beneath its overcoat.

"I concede that you have won your wager, if such it was," said Lord Whitestone. "You had fooled me entirely, Miss Arnet. I did not suspect your secret. What an excellent actress you are."

Marianne fought to keep from shivering and to steady her voice. "You deserved to be tricked for your arrogance," she said. "But I would have told you the truth long ago had it not been for your unreasoning pigheadedness in this matter."

"You say you would have told me," he returned, eyes narrowed. "But how much more dramatic, how better suited to your purpose to have the truth revealed before all of the London *ton*, so that I might be humiliated publicly."

"Do you not think I was humiliated?" she cried, unable to restrain her emotions. "Do you think I enjoyed that scene, with everyone staring at us, looking at me as if I were some sort of freak?"

"Precisely what are you, Marianne Arnet?"

"I used to be an innocent girl who did nothing of which she was ashamed," said Marianne.

"And now?"

"Now, I . . . I feel I have made mistakes but . . . but in all things that matter most, I have done right." She clamped her jaw against her chattering teeth.

"Right?" His tone sharpened. "You call it right to hide a traitor, a spy for the French? Do you want Napoleon to win this war? Do you want our prince, our prime minister to be cut down in the street? Do you call that right?"

"My mother is a very sick woman," Marianne said. "She is incapable of hurting anyone. And she is guilty of no crime save loyalty to her husband."

"Nonsense! She is guilty of treason against the crown of England! And while it may be true that she is ill, she is perfectly capable of wielding a pistol, or of gathering information to pass on to an assassin."

"If you think she is so dangerous and I am protecting her, why did you not have me taken off to prison?" Marianne challenged. "If you loathe and despise me and my family, why should you help us in any particular?" She felt tears swimming to the surface and hoped the darkness would hide them.

Lord Whitestone sat back on his horse and jerked his chin up sharply. "Do you truly want to know why I did not have you hauled off to prison, Marianne?"

"Yes, I do."

"Because if I did, I should be forced to see you again to question you, and it is my devout wish never to lay eyes upon you again. You are a liar, a deceiver, and God knows what else. I have never met so evil or unworthy a woman, and to think that I allowed myself to—" He halted and glared at her.

She could stand no more of this. "Then go! Go away, and I assure you that I have no more desire to see you in future than you have to see me! You are haughty and cold, unjust and too blind to see the truth when it dangles before your own eyes!"

"Then tell me this truth!" She thought she detected a note of pleading in his voice. "If there is some aspect to all this that may put it in another light, I urge you as a loyal British subject to put it before me."

Marianne felt herself wavering. If she told him about her father, would he believe her? If he did, what would he do then? Perhaps he could be trusted now.

"What would you do with such information?" she asked. "If I required that you not reveal it to another soul, would you agree?"

Anger tightened his jaw. "Do you take me for a complete idiot? If there is another aspect to this matter, it must be relayed at once to the prime minister and the Foreign Office. Do you think I would trust anything you, so accomplished a trickster, told me in confidence? You might say the sun rises at night or the rain falls up, and fool me into believing it, and into telling no one who might set me straight. If you have some evidence that might clear your mother, by all means present it, but do not imagine you can lie your way out this time.''

Marianne bit down on the insides of her cheeks to keep from screaming at him. What a stiffhead he was! There might be —almost certainly were—unsuspected French spies still in the highest levels of government, and a word from any of them would mean death to her father.

"Since you will not trust me and you refuse to honour my request for secrecy, I have nothing further to say to you, sir.''

She watched as he reined his horse about and, without another word, rode off down the dark street. Now it was over, and there was no more to be said. This was a rift that would never be mended. He thought her dishonest and dishonourable, even after all he knew of her. Someday the truth would be known, but it would be too late.

A soft nicker roused her, and she glanced at Ginger waiting patiently for her. "Poor horse,'' she said. "I've left you out in the rain, haven't I? I must get you back before you take ill yourself.''

She ducked back into the house and excused herself as rapidly as possible. Ignoring Sarah's and Elizabeth's protests, she dashed back out into the night and, with some difficulty, hauled herself up onto the sidesaddle. There was no sign of Rob, but she couldn't blame him if he had panicked at the sight of the soldiers.

The ride home was an agony of regrets, of anger and chill, of longing and humiliation. Over and over she reenacted in her mind the scene between herself and Lord Whitestone, imagining other words they might have said, how his look might have softened, how he might have taken her tenderly into his arms, how she might have been able to entrust him with her secret. But none of those things had happened, nor ever would happen.

It was a numb and exhausted young lady who arrived some time later at the house in Grosvenor Square. Marianne was grateful that Ginger appeared to know her way home, for otherwise she very much doubted they would have arrived at all.

The groom stared at her in dismay as he handed her down. "You'll catch your death of cold, Miss!" he said. "And it's my fault!"

"Hush." Marianne managed a ghost of a smile. "I saved a life tonight. That was worth everything."

She left him staring after her as she mounted the back stairs unseen and peeled off her tattered clothing in Jane's bedroom. Downstairs, the band played on, and she could hear the faint tinkle of voices. The ball was a huge success and would likely go on for several more hours.

At last Marianne slipped into a clean shift and crawled into bed, only to dream again and again of angry dark eyes, reproaching her.

She awoke to find Jane sleeping alongside of her. From the light glowing through the curtain, Marianne judged it to be mid-morning.

She dressed quietly and went downstairs, to find a grave-looking group at breakfast. Will, lines of weariness around his eyes, sat staring into a cup of coffee, while Grandfather paced angrily along the sideboard.

"What has happened?" Marianne looked from one to another, at her stern-faced Uncle Charles and the pained expressions on the faces of Celia, Edith, and Lucinda. "Why are you all about so early? You must have danced until nearly dawn."

"And the devil take us for it!" said Lord Marlow. "It was not until the guests had gone that Will remembered that Lord Whitestone knew the whereabouts of your mother. We rode out to the house in Boar's Lane but the women there acted quite strange."

"They spoke of soldiers," said Will grimly. "They said your mother had gone, but they would not say where."

Uncle Charles rested his elbows on the table. "I forced my way in and searched for her, but she was not there. It was evident the soldiers had been inside. Their muddy tracks were all about."

"Oh!" It had not occurred to Marianne that the others might go to fetch her mother. She glanced about to be sure there were no servants nearby and then said, "She is at your house, Will."

"What?" Everyone straightened and stared at her.

154

"I—I did not dare delay one moment, so I rode there myself last night, and warned her," Marianne said.

"You rode through London alone at night?" Grandfather exclaimed. "In the rain, unprotected? I will never forgive that cur Whitestone for this, not until the day I die!"

"Mother must be spirited away before they think of searching Will's house," she said. "I hate to see her moved, for she is not well, but we must think of another place."

"My house in Kent!" said Edith. "It was part of my dowry and surely no one will think of searching there. It is near enough, and an elderly couple keeps it quite habitable. I am sure their discretion can be relied upon."

"Excellent," said her husband.

"What if they are watching us?" Marianne protested. "We can scarcely go clumping about to fetch her, the whole lot of us, and expect to pass unobserved."

"The chit is right," said the earl. "Will, you and she and Celia return home in your carriage as you would normally. You will warn Mary and arrange for her things to be packed."

"I fear she has very little," said Marianne.

"My clothes may suit," said Celia. "Very well, Lord Marlow, and then what shall we do?"

He looked thoughtful for a moment before he spoke again. "How many black dresses and veils have you?"

Celia looked puzzled but responded, "I believe we have several. My old nurse, Miss Crane, keeps numerous costumes as well."

"Then we shall do this," said Grandfather. "A short time later other carriages will arrive—mine, and two of Charles's. When they depart, along with whatever vehicles Will possesses, each of them will carry a woman in black, with a veil."

"We shall add our mourning clothes also, so there may be—how many—six of us or so!" said Lucinda. "Mother and I can take the curricle and change our garments at Will's."

The earl nodded. "Very good, and Will, you have a calash, I think? Excellent. How many females have we?"

"There are Marianne and Jane and Lucinda, and Celia and Miss Crane and myself," said Edith. "And Mary, of course."

"You realise, do you not, that we may all be accused of aiding a

155

traitor?'' Lord Marlow warned. "Although I think it unlikely the prince will have the lot of us thrown into prison, it is a possibility."

Edith sighed. "We are already ruined in society," she said. "At least let us thumb our noses at them and have some fun from it."

"Then we are agreed," said Uncle Charles, rising.

"Wait." Marianne turned to her grandfather. "You haven't said how Mother will escape."

"Haven't I?" said Lord Marlow. "Why, you and she will dress as parlourmaids, since you are so expert at disguises, and go walking as if it is your morning off, and take a hackney to meet us at Westminster Bridge. She will transfer to my carriage, which by then no doubt will have been thoroughly inspected by the soldiers."

"You're wonderful!" cried Marianne, throwing her arms around him. "I would never have thought of anything so clever!"

"I'm not so sure about that," said Lord Marlow, wryly. "The only thing I hope is that we are indeed being watched. What a joke it would be on us all to go to such measures and find they had not been needed!"

═15═

THE FACT THAT they were being watched became evident as soon as they ventured outside. Marianne spotted two men lounging about and guessed them to be Bow Street Runners, and a carriage drove suspiciously near theirs all the way home.

It was decided that Marianne should not accompany her mother, for she herself was under too much suspicion and might be readily identified. Furthermore, she was sneezing severely. Miss Crane insisted on being the companion, and this was agreed upon.

Despite the knowledge that her mother might at any moment be snatched off to prison, Marianne could not help but enjoy the sense of excitement in the Sloan household as the Marlows and Sloans converged and set to transforming all the women into black-veiled figures of mystery.

The greatest danger, Marianne felt, was that the enemy—for so she had come to think of their tormenters, although they were in fact only attempting to protect the crown—might close in too soon and search the house. However, apparently somewhat the wiser after their failure the previous night, they had no doubt decided that no one would be so foolish as to display Madame Arnet openly and that a raid would result in finding nothing. Instead, they would watch—while the Marlows and Sloans and Arnets were all to be disguised, just as Marianne had been so many times.

She tried throughout the morning, as they hurried about pinning up hems and restitching veils onto black hats, to keep her thoughts from straying to that tall, arrogant figure on horseback of the previous night. But it was in vain.

Why had he not allowed her to be hauled off to prison? Perhaps he did truly hold her in some affection, or perhaps he had spoken the truth when he said he did not wish to see her again. He had called her a liar and a deceiver, evil and unworthy. Yet he had said that he had allowed himself to . . . to what? The words had been broken off there. Not to fall in love, surely, but perhaps to wish an attachment of some sort.

Certainly not an honourable one, Marianne told herself. Perhaps he had thought to make her Serena Brinoli's successor. Well, that false Italian from Liverpool could have the man if she wished. If only the thought did not send such painful spasms through Marianne's heart!

They set off in their various vehicles to their sundry destinations. Grandfather's carriage, carrying Edith, was to rendezvous with Will's calash, carrying Lucinda, in Bond Street, where the pair planned to do some shopping. The Marlow curricle was to take Grandfather and Marianne to Marlow House, and the Marlow carriage was to transport Jane to the house of a friend she wished to visit. That left the Sloan carriage for Charles and Celia, who were to meet Miss Crane and Mary at Westminster and take her to Kent. Will was to remain at home in case there were any inquiries.

The soldiers and runners, as might be expected, saw something rather strange in so many carriages setting off at such an early hour, and ruthlessly stopped and searched each of them. Marianne's heart pounded as she was ordered to lift her veil, but it was quickly seen that she was much too young to be Madame Arnet.

Edith had a difficult moment, as Marianne later learned, for she was of an age with Mary, and it seemed for a spell that she might be ordered off to prison. At last an officer rode by who thought he recognised her, and her identity was soon confirmed by none other than Lord Whitestone. He apologised for the intrusion and she snubbed him roundly, she related later with considerable glee.

In all the muddle, no one noticed the two parlourmaids who set out sedately on a walk, and so the rendezvous was made, and Mary Arnet taken safely out of London.

The family dined together at Marlow House, drinking several toasts to the success of their scheme. Only Marianne seemed in low spirits, which were attributed to her having contracted a cold.

Jane took her hand quietly as they sat next to each other. "I know how badly you must feel," she whispered. "But he is not worthy of you."

Marianne nodded miserably and wished she could share that conviction.

After dinner, when the gentlemen had finished their cigars and joined the ladies in the drawing room, Marianne asked her grandfather quietly if she might return to Wiltshire as soon as possible.

"You cannot mean to flee now!" he said. "You do not mean you care for what society may think?"

"Not at all," she said. "But I have imposed on Will and Celia long enough."

"Then you shall stay here," said Edith. "Do you know, we had a number of calling cards left today, far more than I should have expected. And do you know whose was among them? Sir Edward Beamish! How do you like that? I knew he was taken with Jane."

"There was one from a certain Mr. Falmby as well," murmured Lucinda, and Marianne smiled.

"It isn't what you think," she told the others. "It's only that I feel a need to be alone for a while. In a month or two, perhaps I shall be entirely restored. You need not come away, Grandfather, but do say I may go."

"Nonsense," said Lord Marlow. "I have no wish to stay here." He paused, and from the glow on his face, Marianne suspected he was remembering his joyful reunion that morning with his daughter, their hugs and cries and great happiness at being reconciled. "No, now that my daughter is not in London, I think I shall retire as well."

All that evening, against all sense and judgement, Marianne found herself listening for the sound of carriage wheels. If only Lord Whitestone would come on some pretext or other. But where could it lead? He was surely as intransigent as ever, and furious at having been duped that day, for he must have known their stratagem had been designed to protect Lady Mary and had succeeded.

Marianne spent a last night at the Sloans' and then took a tearful leave of Will and Celia and Fritzella, with whom she had shared so many adventures. They promised earnestly to write, and

Miss Crane took her aside briefly to say, "I have read your fortune again, my dear."

"What did you find?"

"There are many obstacles still before you," said the old woman. "But you will come clear in the end."

Marianne nodded and turned away to hide her pain. In the end, perhaps she might marry some gentleman of whom she would be fond, and that would be coming out well enough. But would she ever forget that high-cheeked, proud face and the way his eyes sometimes softened when he looked at her?

She and Grandfather departed together in comfortable silence. It was quite late when they reached home, but it looked ever so welcome, the massive Gothic house with its arched gateway and the yellow-grey stones of the courtyard.

The next few days passed quietly. Marianne spent much of her time in the garden, gazing at the primroses and violets of early spring, wondering how long it took a heart to heal and how one might exorcise from one's mind the image of a man who was both one's love and one's enemy.

She had letters from Jane and Lucinda bearing good news. Both Sir Edward and Mr. Falmby were pressing their suits, and it appeared that her cousins might be married before summer's end. Through Sir Edward, Jane had some news of Lord Whitestone. He had left London for a destination unknown, she wrote; even Ned was quite at a loss as to where his friend might have gone. The search for Madame Arnet was given up as hopeless, and although an additional spy was captured, he was able to shed no light on the matter.

She wrote back to them as cheerfully as she could, and sent a letter to Will and Celia, enclosing a new poem she had written.

> Spring has sailed home again, a sapling for its mast:
> Above's a morning cloud, soft as a sail unfurled.
> One seaman that I know from voyages long past
> Has not come back; he skims across the world

Upon another ship, that leaps to his commands.
Here the spring sky's bright as any sunlit sea,
And cargo's safely brought: spice from distant lands,
And mint, hybiscus, comfrey, rose hips ripe for tea.

But I leave empty-handed and, seeking what was mine,
Must navigate alone the empty sea of time.

Miss Crane wrote also, with news that was at least distracting. Elizabeth had married a tradesman, who knew about her chequered past but forgave her, while Libby Holcomb, the erstwhile companion of Sir Edward, had joined Miss Crane's household on Boar's Lane and was proving herself quite talented as a seamstress.

The most interesting news concerned Serena Brinoli. That woman, whom Miss Crane insisted on referring to as Martha Bowkes, had fallen in love with a man who operated a travelling circus. Miss Crane had seen her last at Greenwich Fair, displaying a lion in a cage to Cockney boys with dirty faces, and demonstrating to sailors a learned pig said to be able to cipher and spell.

Just as the year turned to April, a messenger came from London, racing so hard that horse and rider were drenched in sweat as they thundered into the courtyard. Marianne, who saw them arrive from the morning-room window, clenched her hands into fists, praying there was no bad news of her parents.

She hurried into the hall to find Grandfather beaming with delight. "Good news, Marianne!" he cried. "Paris has surrendered behind Napoleon's back. Now he is sure to agree to a treaty. The war will be over in a matter of days!"

"But . . ." She hesitated to continue before the messenger, and the earl, perceiving this, paid the man and sent him down to the kitchen for refreshment.

"But what of Father?" she asked when he had departed. "Has he left France? Is his part in this known?"

Grandfather shook his head. "There has been no word. It may be that he cannot leave Paris yet. There is still fighting in France, you know."

"Mother must be in agony," Marianne said. "I wish I could go to her."

"It yet could be dangerous," Lord Marlow cautioned. "I should like to see her again too, but we had best wait."

Later that day, as she sat in her bedroom, Marianne thought she heard more hoofbeats from the front of the house. However, when she went down a short time later, there was no one there.

"Was there another message, Grandfather?" she asked, entering his study timidly, for it was a heavily masculine room, with dark woods and leather, into which she rarely ventured.

"Another message? No," he said.

"I thought I heard a horse."

"Must have been the messenger from this morning riding off," he said, and she nodded dubiously.

The next few days were tense ones. Letters came from her cousins: Lucinda was now betrothed to Mr. Falmby, and was happy to report that Priscilla Land, having been deserted by all her suitors owing to her wicked tongue and unkind nature, had bestowed her hand on the odious Mr. Horace Trimble.

Jane had some news of Lord Whitestone, although she said his behaviour continued to puzzle his friends. He had returned to town for a brief period, conferred with officials in the Foreign Office and then ridden away again without leaving word as to where he might be found.

Meanwhile, Marianne attempted to work on a book of poetry, which her grandfather had agreed to underwrite. In her anxious state, however, her muse seemed to have deserted her.

At last came the news Marianne had been waiting for: Her father had reached England, and his greatly relieved connexions in the Foreign Office were free at last to reveal the truth. So the whole business of *L'affaire Arnet* was revealed as the counter-espionage effort it had been all along.

Monsieur Arnet had gone to join his wife in Kent, and sent his love to his daughter and father-in-law but begged their indulgence while he and Lady Mary enjoyed a few days alone together. Then, his wife's health being much restored, they planned to travel to Wiltshire.

"All has come right, just as it ought," said the earl, pouring them both a glass of sherry to celebrate. "I have a brave daughter and son-in-law, and an equally brave granddaughter. Had you not ridden as you had, that monster Whitestone would have clapped her in prison, and she should have been dead by now."

"I wonder," Marianne said. "Had he been told the whole story, would he have persisted in believing the worst of us?"

"I've no doubt of it," said Lord Marlow. "A more thick-skulled rogue I've yet to encounter."

Marianne excused herself as soon as she could without dampening her grandfather's happiness. She wandered out to her favourite corner of the garden, where she sat surrounded by hedges of primroses.

By now, Lord Whitestone must know the truth. But he had neither called her nor written to her, and even if he did so now, how could she ever trust him? Anyone might praise and admire the Arnets now, but any man who loved her would have known long before that she was incapable of treason.

═16═

THE ARNETS ARRIVED sooner than expected. As their coach pulled up before the great pillared portico, Marianne peered through the velvet curtains in indecision, wanting to run out to greet them and at the same time suddenly shy.

She followed Grandfather to the front door, half-hiding behind his large frame. Still, she had a clear view of her father, a man she would scarcely have recognised, limping up the walk.

She remembered him as tall and portly, with an air that at the time she had thought was sophistication but which she had later, not knowing the truth about him, believed furtive. Now she knew it was caution that had kept her father from straightforward ways, for he smiled broadly and openly at the sight of her. He was not so tall as she had thought when a child, and much thinner. As she darted forward at last to be encircled and pressed against him, she thought in surprise that he seemed almost frail.

Beside him, Lady Mary glowed with happiness, and she and Marianne embraced joyfully. Both parents slipped their arms about their daughter's waist as the threesome walked up to join the earl.

There was much to discuss: how Jean-Pierre had escaped before Boney learned of his treachery and could send an assassin; the abdication of the emperor himself and the plans to sign a treaty; the future of France, and whether Napoleon would be executed, imprisoned or exiled.

Gradually, as they relaxed in each other's company, the conversation turned to more personal matters. Jean-Pierre already knew of Marianne's escapades in London and how she had saved her mother, but there were other matters to catch up on. Marianne told them freely of her friendship with Will and her writing, and revealed that she had been published in the *Gazette*.

"What a surprising *jeune fille* you are," said her father admiringly.

Marianne escorted her mother upstairs and the two sat on the edge of Lady Mary's bed for a chat.

"There is something I think you have not told me," said the older woman after glancing in the wardrobe to see that the maid had hung her new clothes properly.

"What, Mother?"

"You have told us how you tricked Lord Whitestone, and made a fool of him before society," said Lady Mary. "Yet I could not help but notice, for all my fear of him, that he is a most handsome man, and from all that is said he apparently grew somewhat attached to you."

Marianne stared down at the flowered carpet, wishing her mother were not quite so perceptive.

"There is no need to speak of it if you do not wish," Lady Mary said.

Marianne looked up at her. "Oh, Mother, you're right," she said. "I did become fond of him too. But it's hopeless."

"Because you humiliated him? Men are rather proud creatures, I believe."

"Yes, and . . . I don't think he really loved me. Once he learned who I was, he wanted no more to do with me."

"He thought you were aiding a traitor."

"He should have known better!"

"Perhaps," said her mother.

"You can't mean that I should . . . should go back to London and seek him out?" For a moment, Marianne wondered if she should do exactly that, but Lady Mary shook her head.

"That would not answer," she said. "I fear in our society it is the gentleman who must make the first move, or your reputation would be ruined."

"He will never do that," sighed Marianne.

Her mother laid an arm about her shoulders. "I am sorry that your first experience with love should have been an unhappy one, and that it was because of us."

"It was worth it," Marianne said more bravely than she felt. "I wouldn't have had you otherwise. And it's all come right in the end.''

But she returned to her room feeling deeply depressed. Try as she might, she could not stop thinking about the marquis. Jeremy. She lay back on her bed and his face immediately appeared before her, with that puzzled, delighted look he had so often worn when he gazed at her. How well they had suited together, how much they had shared the same sense of humour, the same joy in life. Under other circumstances . . .

If I thought he did love me, I would go to London and seek him out, Marianne thought. But I couldn't bear to be spurned.

He was probably this very minute preparing for a ball, where he would hold another woman in his arms as they danced, talked, and laughed. A cruel fist of pain tightened around Marianne's heart.

"Miss?" There was a rap at the door.

"Come in, Dora." She sat up as the maid opened the door timidly.

"There's this come for you in the mail," the young woman said, handing an envelope to her with a curtsey and then scurrying out.

Marianne looked at the thick letter, noting that it bore Will's handwriting, and opened it.

Inside was a letter from her cousin, and another envelope. It was addressed to Mata, in Lord Whitestone's handwriting.

Half-frozen with apprehension, she felt her hands move clumsily over the enclosure, tearing it a little as she opened it and withdrew the letter.

"My dear Mata," it said. "I had hoped to hear from you before now, although I cannot complain, for you had warned that you would be from home. I myself shall be going away for some time. It is my intent to spend several years on the Continent and perhaps even journey to India."

He was going away! A sense of loss ate through Marianne as she read further.

"I fear the romance of which I wrote you earlier has come to a sorry end because of my own folly. I need not tell you the particulars, for it is my intent now to reveal my name, since if we are to continue our correspondence it will be necessary for you to write me at the various residences where I may lodge. I am Jeremy Hanbridge, Marquis of Whitestone, and all of England must know by now how I wronged the lovely and desirable Miss Marianne Arnet."

She swallowed a lump in her throat. Perhaps there was hope after all. But he had said he was departing and, further, it still pained her that he had come to value her only after learning that her parents were heroes rather than traitors. Had the truth never been revealed, she would still have been the same person. How could love be built on anything less than trust and unwavering faith in one another?

She continued reading, savouring each word despite her anguish. "I have tried several times to see her, but her grandfather has refused me entrance, and I cannot blame him. I have written as well, but the letters have been returned unread.

"I am leaving this letter at the *Gazette* and then I shall return to Wiltshire and attempt to see Miss Arnet once again. Failing that, I must conclude that she has no wish to see me, and I shall be leaving for the Continent.

"If you wish to continue our correspondence, I beg you to write to me at once. I shall be staying at the Fox and Hounds, just outside Wootton Bassett." There followed his signature.

Marianne dropped the letter into her lap. He was here in Wiltshire, and he wished to see her.

Thoughts vied for attention in her head. He had come to the house, and Grandfather had turned him away. He had written, but Grandfather had sent back the letters. He loved her enough to seek her again, despite Grandfather's opposition and the jokes that would be made at his expense in London were this devotion known. Surely it must be enough that he loved her now, even though he had not loved her sufficiently to believe in her before.

Marianne stared down at her clenched hands. Oh, Jeremy, what shall I do? she asked silently. I do not think I can bear to let you go away.

Something tickled at the edge of her memory and she frowned. She had heard a horse in the courtyard. When had that been? The day the messenger arrived. But which messenger? Now it came back more clearly. It had been the news of the surrender of Paris.

But we did not know then that Father was safe, she thought. If we didn't know, then the truth hadn't been revealed yet, so Jeremy couldn't have known.

It must have been his horse she had heard, for now that she searched her memory, she was almost certain she had heard hoofs arriving and departing, yet Grandfather had tried to persuade her she had heard only the messenger leaving. Had it been anyone else, why should he have lied?

Jeremy had come as soon as it was clear the war was about to end, as soon as he had been able in good conscience to leave his duties in London. He had come before he knew that the Arnets were not traitors.

Marianne jumped to her feet. She must go to him at once! She hesitated only briefly. Grandfather would never allow it, but she need not tell him.

She bit her lip to curb a smile as an idea struck her. The very thing!

She dug through her wardrobe until she found an old dark-grey round gown from her schoolroom days. She changed rapidly into it and added an apron that she used for berrying, tucking her hair under a mobcap. Surveying herself in the mirror, she decided she would make a passable serving wench.

Marianne folded the letter into her pocket and slipped out the door and down the back stairs. It was an easy matter to have a groom saddle up her horse, for no one expected her to dress in her best riding habit merely to hack about the countryside.

She set off eagerly, but by the time the three-quarter-hour journey passed, her anticipation had given way to apprehension. True, he had come here to see her, and presumably his intentions were honourable, but he might find that once in her presence he was more angry than pleased. Perhaps he had lied to Mata, and his real motivation was something else—to win her heart and break it, as she had seemingly done with his, or to . . .

Marianne, for all her fears, was hard put to find any good reason why the marquis would have come unless he truly cared for her. Still, her skeptical mind would not give her peace. Perhaps he had left already and was on his way to the Continent.

She arrived at the Fox and Hounds in a state of nervous excitement, and was quickly faced with the problem of how she was to go about announcing herself.

The taproom was empty of customers for it was still a bit before teatime, and Marianne wandered back toward the kitchen. She had come here several times with Grandfather and, prior to that, had lived not far away with the Sloans. Their former cook had gone to work for the inn, and she kept her fingers crossed in hopes that the woman was still here. Mabel, that had been her name, Mabel Cormany.

Marianne was dismayed, on entering the kitchen, to find only a serving girl and a table boy, but they nodded when she asked for Mrs. Cormany, and that person soon appeared.

"Why, if it ain't Marianne Arnet!" she cried. "What be you doing here, and dressed like that?"

"It's all in fun, Mrs. Cormany," Marianne said. "There's a gentleman staying here who's a friend of our family, only he doesn't know that I know he's here. I thought it would be a bit of a joke if I took him his tea."

Mrs. Cormany nodded, and Marianne was grateful that she'd always been a jolly woman with a good sense of humour. "Now, who is this gentleman?"

"Lord Whitestone."

The serving girl whistled. "Coo, that's a fine one."

"I guess there's no harm in it," Mrs. Cormany said. "Just bide a bit, and we'll have his tray ready. He takes it in his room most days, and I expect he'll be doing the same today."

Most days, Marianne thought with a pang. He has been here a while then, just as he said. And he hasn't gone yet. Poor Jeremy, if he really does love me, he has been ill used.

It seemed an eternity but was in fact only a quarter of an hour before the tea-tray was ready, with an appetising array of sandwiches and cakes. It took Marianne a moment to get the feel of carrying it, but she balanced it quickly on her shoulder and, with a quick bit of tutoring from Mrs. Cormany, carried it up the back stairs in proper style.

She swallowed hard and then rapped cautiously on Lord Whitestone's door.

"Who is it?" The familiar voice, despite its slightly annoyed tone, sent a thrill down her back.

"I've brought your tea, your lordship," she said in as good an imitation as she could manage of a serving-girl's voice.

"Very well. Bring it in then."

She swung the door open and entered. The room was a pleasant one, large, with a four-poster bed, print curtains on the window, and a faded rug on the floor. The marquis sat with his back to her at a writing table, penning some sort of note.

"Just leave it on the side table there," he said without looking up.

She did as he instructed, finding it a bit awkward to shift the heavy tray from her shoulder to her hands but managing without clinking the china more than a little.

She turned and waited, but still he took no notice of her. "Will that be all, sir?" she asked.

"Yes, thank you, Miss. You may go."

A smile tugged at the corners of her mouth while worried butterflies danced in her stomach. "Are you quite sure that will be all, sir?"

"Isn't that what I—" He turned around and stopped with his plumed pen in midair. "Good God. Marianne!"

"You're going to drop ink on your coat if you're not careful," she said.

"What? Oh." He returned the pen to the inkstand and hurried to his feet. "What are you doing here? How did you know where I was?"

She caught her hands together in front of her to keep them from trembling. "Jeremy, did you really try to see me before you knew my father was working for England?"

He nodded slowly. "Yes. I—I was so angry at first, but then when I got to thinking about it, I missed you so much I could hardly bear it."

"Is that all?"

"I don't understand."

She took a deep breath. "Did you really think I would be a traitor to my own country, even for my parents' sakes?"

He shook his head. "No. What a fool I felt. Had I stopped to think, I'd have remembered how your mother looked, how ill she was and how delicate. To think she had any role in an attempt to kill the prince was preposterous. I was wrong about a number of other things as well."

"I suppose I can understand it," she said softly. "A lot of your men died on the Peninsula, and you thought my father was partly to blame."

"But I was unfair to you, and all the while you were very brave to aid your mother as you did." He moved toward her, and she shuddered deliciously at his nearness as he reached to take her hands in his. "I suppose some part of me knew you were innocent; that's why I couldn't let them take you off to prison. Marianne, does your coming here mean I'm forgiven? Do I dare to hope that you might consent to be my wife?"

Marianne's heart seemed to swell within her. He wanted to marry her! She nodded, momentarily speechless, and then managed to gasp out, "Yes. Oh, Jeremy!"

Then her arms were around his neck, and he held her by the waist, and they kissed with probing urgency. This time there was no need to hold back, and Marianne revelled in the pressure of his hard body and the joy of exploring his mouth with hers.

She luxuriated in his touch, the firmness of his hands as they played up her back and then gripped her shoulders. She pressed her cheek against his, nuzzling his ear.

At last they stepped apart reluctantly.

"This is quite improper, you know," teased Jeremy. "You alone with me in my room."

"But if we're betrothed, who would object?" she said lightly.

He reached over to touch a strand of her pale hair that had come loose. "That cap suits you," he said. "Do you intend, when we are married, to go about dressed as a servant? I half think I'd like it."

Marianne laughed. "I shall have to dip into Miss Crane's costume box from time to time, just to keep my hand in."

Then his expression sobered. "Do you think your grandfather will consent to the marriage?"

She thought for a moment. "Perhaps not at first, but I know my mother harbours no hard feelings, and I think my father will agree. After a bit, Grandfather will give us his blessing too, I think. He may quite enjoy the irony of it, when he's given it some thought."

"But how did you know where I was?" Jeremy asked, curving

his hand along her cheek. "I don't believe I mentioned it to Lord Marlow, and I hadn't realised you knew of my visits."

"I didn't." She reached into her apron pocket and withdrew the letter. "I learned it from this."

He stared at the sheet of paper in amazement, taking it in his hand and turning it about. "How did you come into possession of this? Do you know Mata, then?"

"Intimately," Marianne said. "Mata is a name made of initials—initials for Marianne Therese Arnet."

Lord Whitestone began to chuckle. "How amazing you are! Then you have been Mata all along? You wrote those splendid poems and those letters?"

"Yes, although I did try to stop them, after you wrote that I wasn't to come to London," Marianne said.

"So that was why Mata broke off our correspondence," he said. "The suddenness of her change in plans seemed rather odd, I must say."

"I would apologise, for I have been reading your thoughts since then, which you sent to her," said Marianne. "But were it not for your continuing to write, I should not be here now."

"That would be unthinkable." There was a gleam in his eye as he bent down to kiss her again, lingeringly. He looked up at last, only to say, "I have never been so thoroughly hoaxed by a woman before, and could never have believed I should enjoy it so much."

"The pleasure, my lord, is mine, I assure you," she said, and stood on tiptoe to receive another kiss.